ESSENTIAL SIGHT-SINGING

MIXED VOICES

VOLUME 1

By Emily Crocker and John Leavitt

CHAPTER 1
1   Beat and Rhythm; Basic Notation; Measures, Meters & Barlines

CHAPTER 2
8   Pitch, Scale & Key of C

CHAPTER 3
14   Whole Steps and Half Steps

CHAPTER 4
19   Sharps and Flats; Key of G Major

CHAPTER 5
25   Accidentals and Key Signature; Rests

CHAPTER 6
34   Melodic Intervals; Harmonic Intervals

CHAPTER 7
44   Tonic Chord

CHAPTER 8
53   Key of F Major

CHAPTER 9
58   Eighth Notes and Rests

CHAPTER 10
66   Changing Meters

APPENDIX
78   Solfège; Numbers; Counting Systems; Simple Meter; Compound Meter

HAL•LEONARD® CORPORATION

7777 W. BLUEMOUND RD. P.O. BOX 13819 MILWAUKEE, WI 53213

Copyright © 2005 by HAL LEONARD CORPORATION
International Copyright Secured   All Rights Reserved

For all works contained herein:
Unauthorized copying, arranging, adapting, recording or public performance is an infringement of copyright.
Infringers are liable under the law.

Visit Hal Leonard Online at
www.halleonard.com

PREFACE

Essential Sight-Singing was adapted from the *Essential Musicianship* books from the *Essential Elements for Choir* choral textbook series in order to bring the most successful aspects of the program into the hands of more choral singers.

It is designed to provide a basis for developing music literacy within the choral rehearsal through sequential development of music reading skills. Choirs are encouraged to spend 10–15 minutes per hour of rehearsal, including practice/review and introducing new material.

Choirs and singers are encouraged to use a systematic method for sight-reading pitch and rhythm. Several methods are outlined in the appendix of this volume.

For pitch reading:
    Solfège (movable do)
    Solfège (fixed do)
    Numbers

For rhythm reading:
    Kodály
    Traditional
    Eastman System

Choose the method based on the age/experience of the singers, methods used by other organizations in your school or district, methods familiar to your students, or your own background or training. Remember, it is not *which* method you use, but rather that it is employed consistently and regularly.

The exercises and songs in this volume are structured to allow students to discover their individual potential. The material is score oriented so that students are led to discover the meaning of music both through experiencing it and interpreting it through the medium of the printed page. This process of converting symbol to sound and sound to symbol is at the heart of becoming a musically literate individual.

Also available is an Accompaniment CD that provides light accompaniment for the combinable pitch builders, speech choruses and songs. In keeping with the spirit of sight-reading, there is no singing on the CD. Unless otherwise noted, starting pitches and one full measure of beats are provided before each pitch builder and a cappella song.

Good luck!

~Emily Crocker and John Leavitt, authors

CHAPTER 1

1.1 Beat and Rhythm

Rhythm is the organization of sound length (duration).

Beat is a steadily recurring pulse.

Rhythm Practice
Practice keeping a steady beat as a group. Clap, tap, or chant with a clock or metronome.

Note Values
Three common note values are the *quarter note*, the *half note*, and the *whole note*.

Quarter Note   Half Note   Whole Note

In most of the music that we'll begin with, the quarter note will be assigned the beat.

You'll notice from the chart below that *two quarter notes* have the same duration as *one half note*, and that *two half notes* (or four quarter notes) have the same duration as *one whole note*.

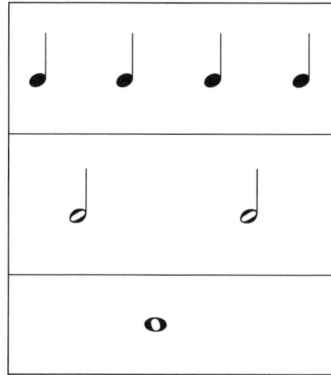

1.2 Rhythm Builder

Read each line (clap, tap, or chant). Concentrate on keeping a steady beat. Repeat as necessary until you've mastered the exercise.

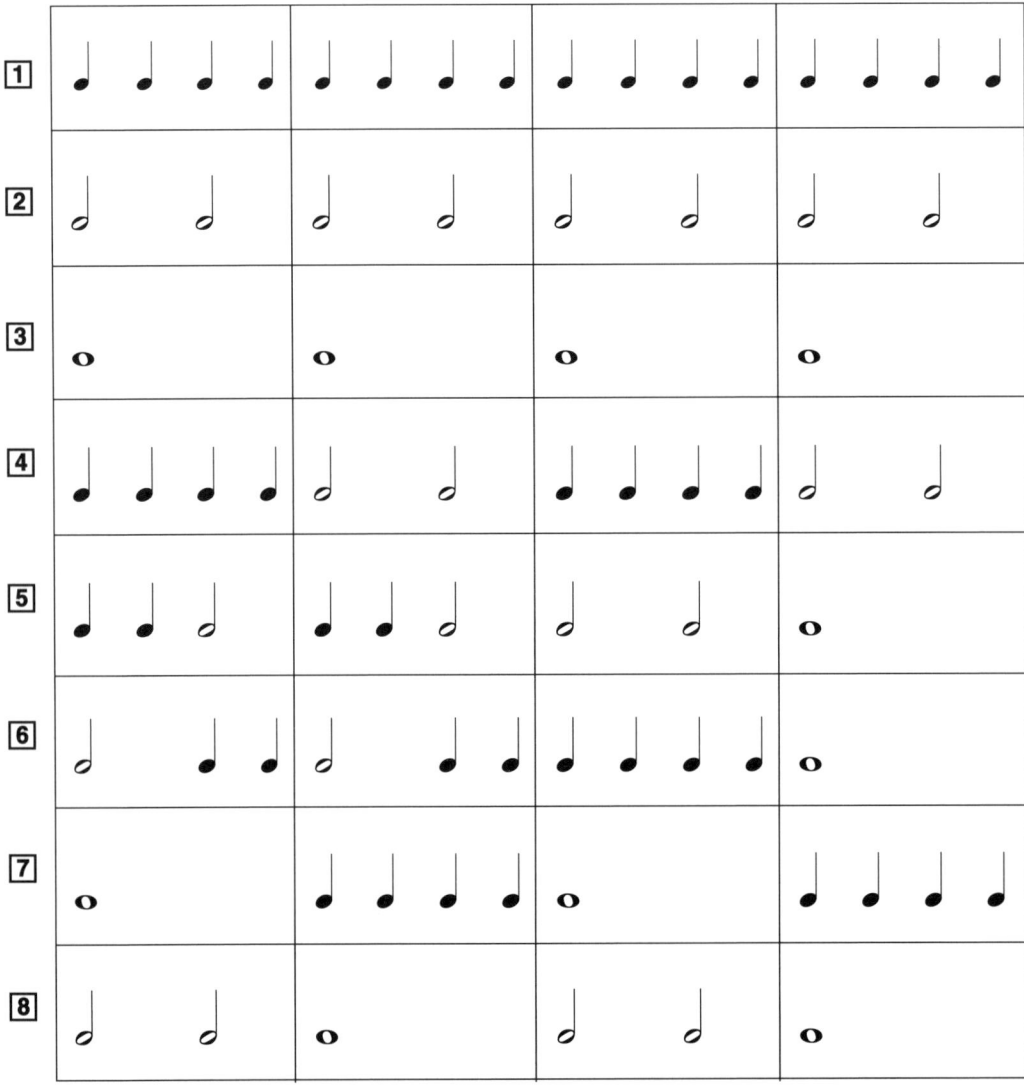

1.3 Basic Notation

A *staff* is a graph of 5 lines and 4 spaces on which music is written. The staff shown below is a grand staff. A *grand staff* is a grouping of two staves.

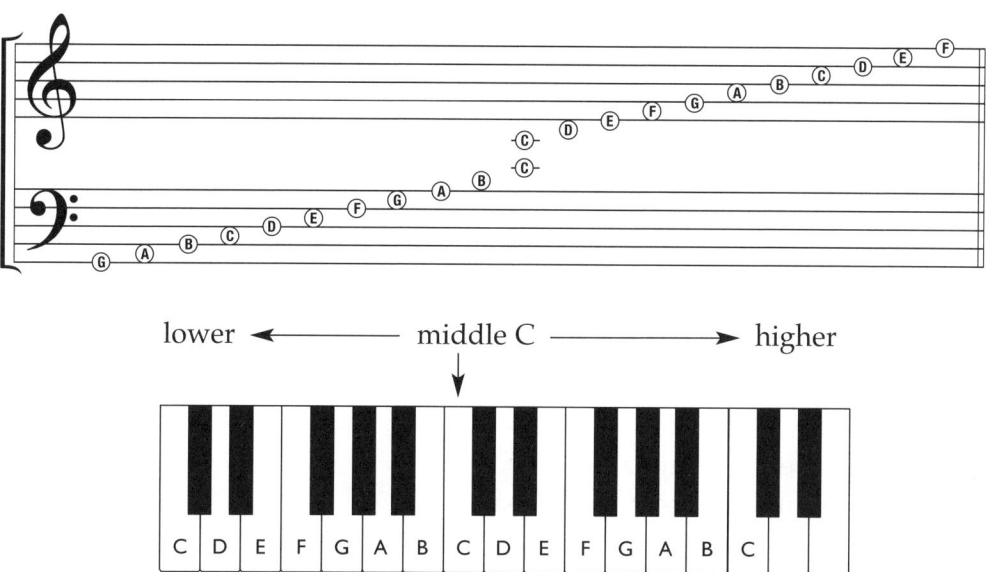

Notice the two symbols at the beginning of the staves on the left hand side. These are called clefs. A *clef* is a symbol that identifies a set of pitches. The *Treble Clef* generally refers to pitches higher than middle C. The *Bass Clef* generally refers to pitches lower than middle C. Notice that middle C has its own little line and may be written in either clef – either at the bottom of the treble clef or the top of the bass clef.

   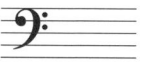

Treble Clef (G Clef)
Second line is G
(The curve of the clef
loops around the G line).

Bass Clef (F Clef)
Fourth line is F
(The dots of the clef
surround the F line).

1.4 Measures, Meters & Barlines

Barlines are vertical lines that divide the staff into smaller sections called *measures*. A *double barline* indicates the end of a section or piece of music.

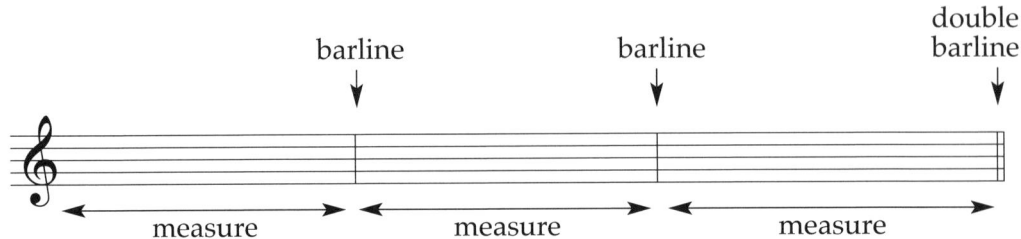

Meter is a form of rhythmic organization. For example:

4 = Four beats per measure (♩ ♩ ♩ ♩).
4 = The quarter note (♩) receives the beat.

3 = Three beats per measure (♩ ♩ ♩).
4 = The quarter note (♩) receives the beat.

2 = Two beats per measure (♩ ♩).
4 = The quarter note (♩) receives the beat.

The numbers that identify the meter are called the *time signature*. The time signature is placed after the clef at the beginning of a song or section of a song.

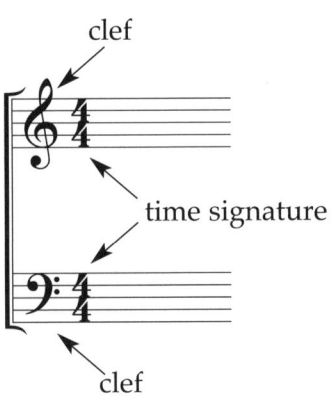

1.5 Rhythm Builder

Read each line (clap, tap, or chant).

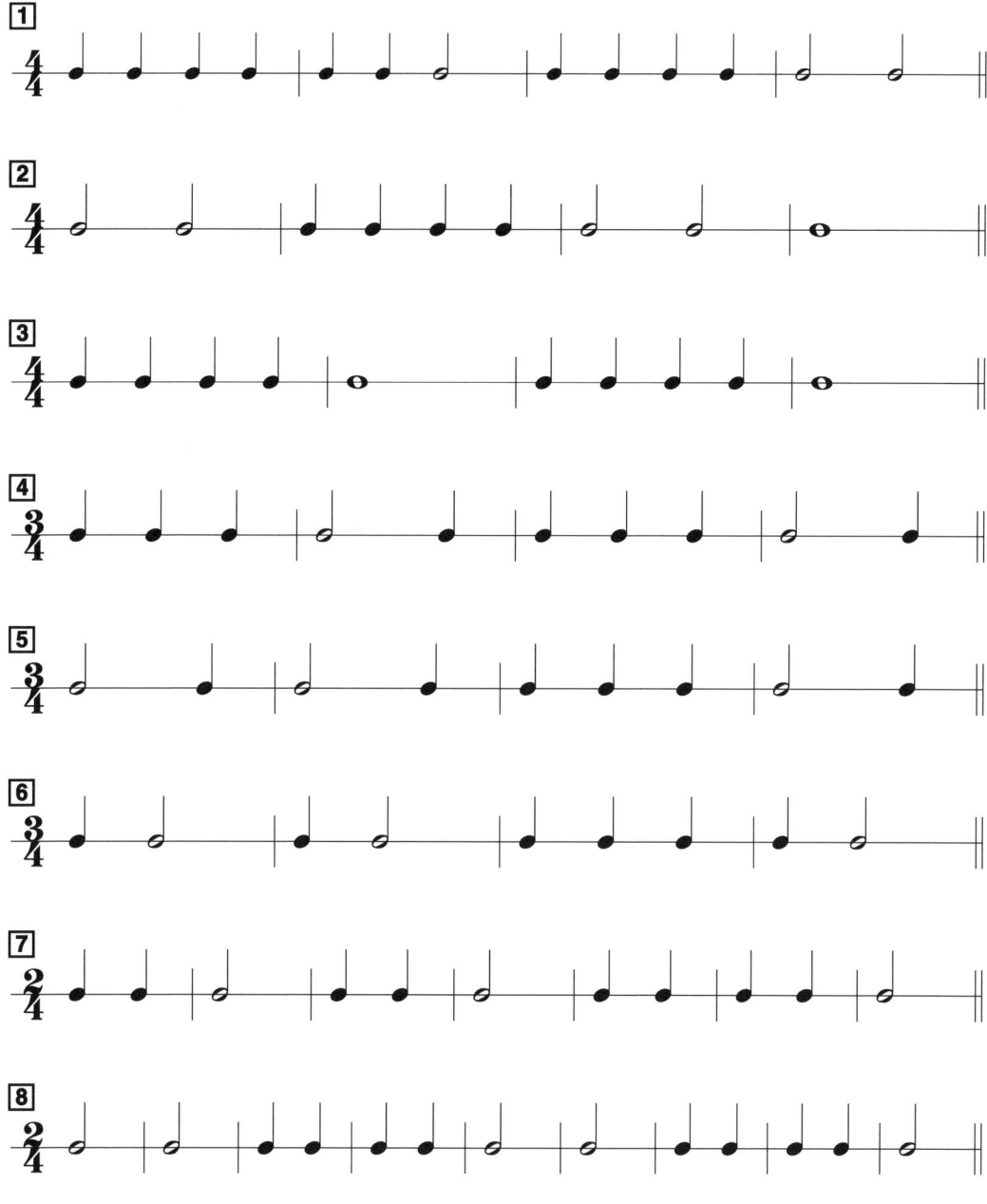

1.6 Pitch Builder

Echo sing or sing as a group.

1.7 Sight-Read

Sight-read the rhythm of these speech choruses. Repeat with the printed text.

Tr. #1 The Months of the Year

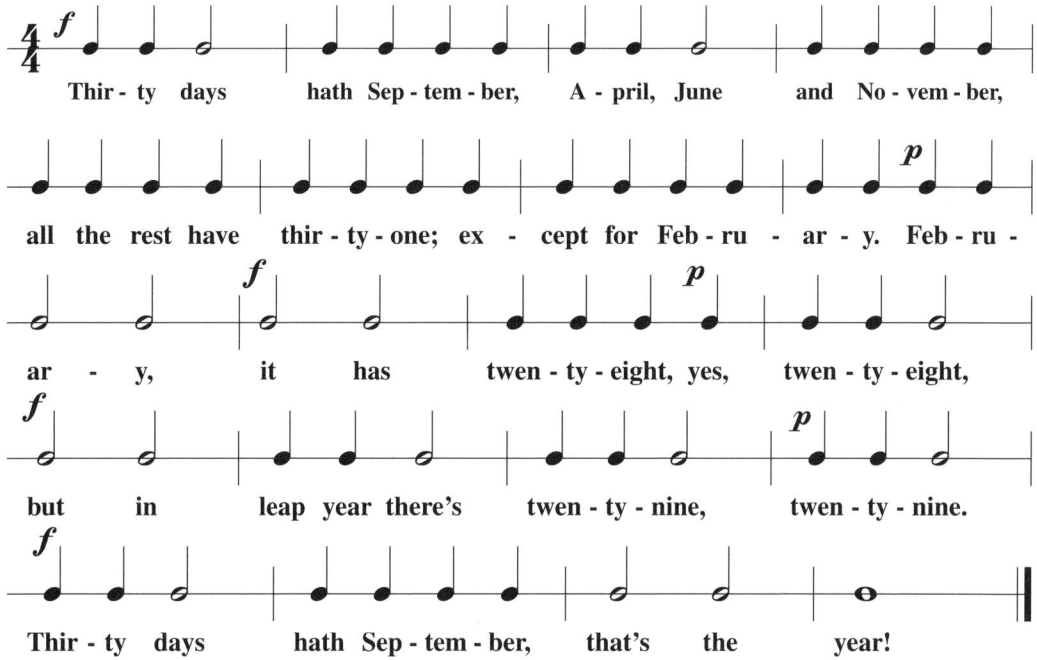

Tr. #2 Tongue Twister

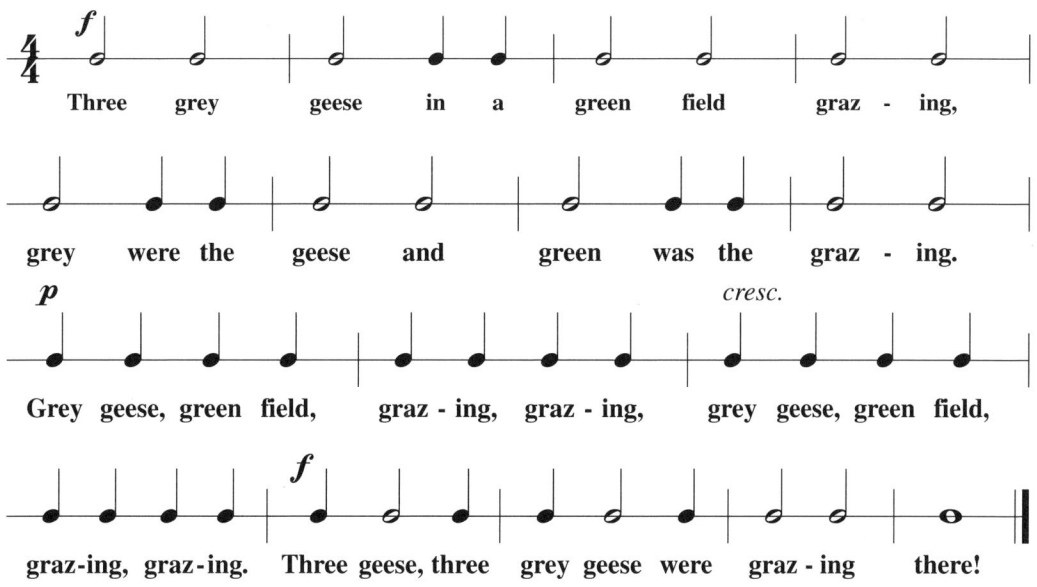

CHAPTER 2

2.1 Pitch, Scale & Key of C

Pitch – The highness or lowness of musical sound.

Scale – An inventory or collection of pitches. The word "scale" (from the Italian *scala*) means "ladder." Thus, many musical scales are a succession of pitches higher and lower.

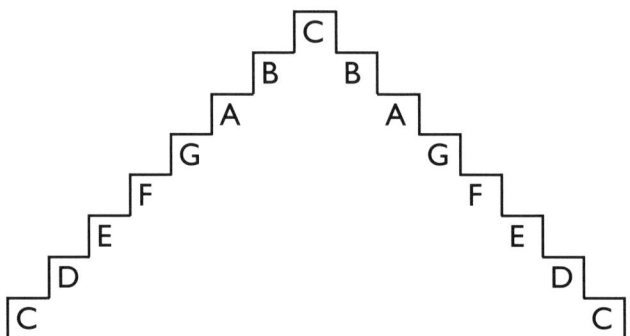

Key – The importance of one pitch over the others in a scale. Frequently, the keynote or tone might be described as the home tone. In the key of C, C is the home tone or keynote.

Key of C Scale

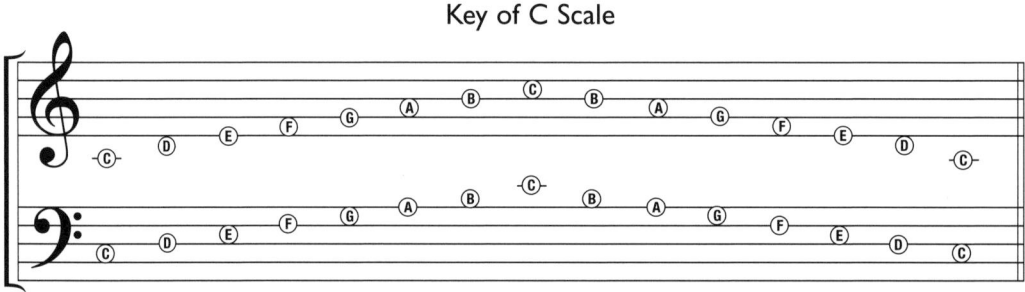

2.2 Pitch Builder

Identify the following pitches in the key of C. Echo sing or sing as a group.

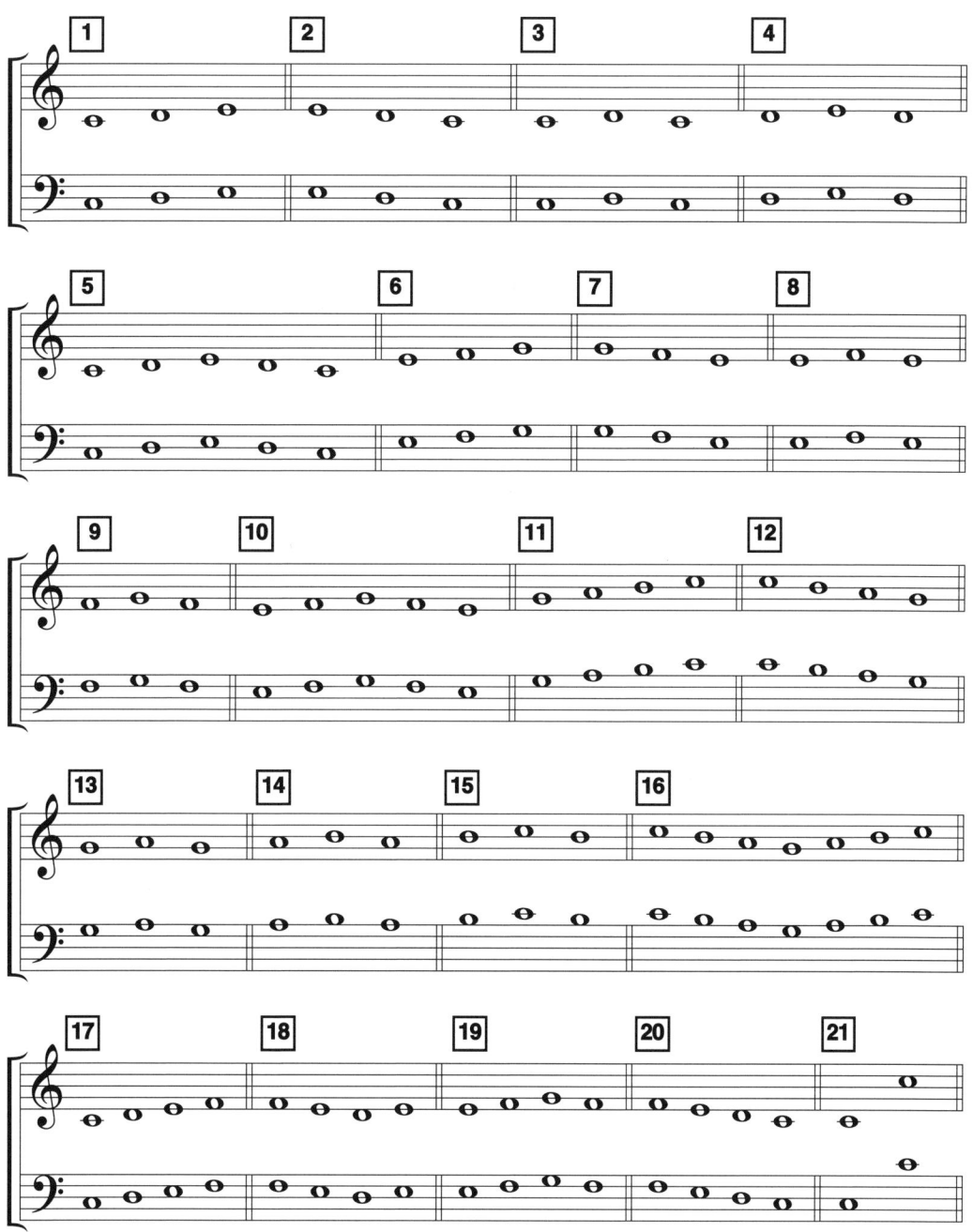

2.3 Pitch Builder

The following exercises combine pitch and rhythm. Chant the rhythm first, then add pitch. Repeat as necessary. When you've mastered all the exercises, you may sing the lines in any combination. For example, divide into two groups with one group singing #1 and the other group singing #2.

Each line sung by itself produces *melody* (a succession of musical tones). When two or more melodies are combined, the result is *harmony* (musical tones sounded simultaneously).

2.4 Sight-Read

Apply what you've learned about music reading to these short songs.
- Chant the rhythm.
- Add pitch. Repeat as necessary for accuracy.
- Sing with text and expression.

Proverbs
для 2-Part Mixed, a cappella

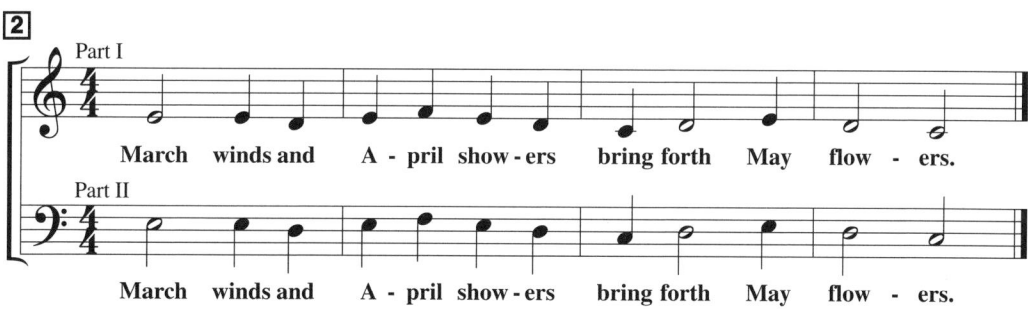

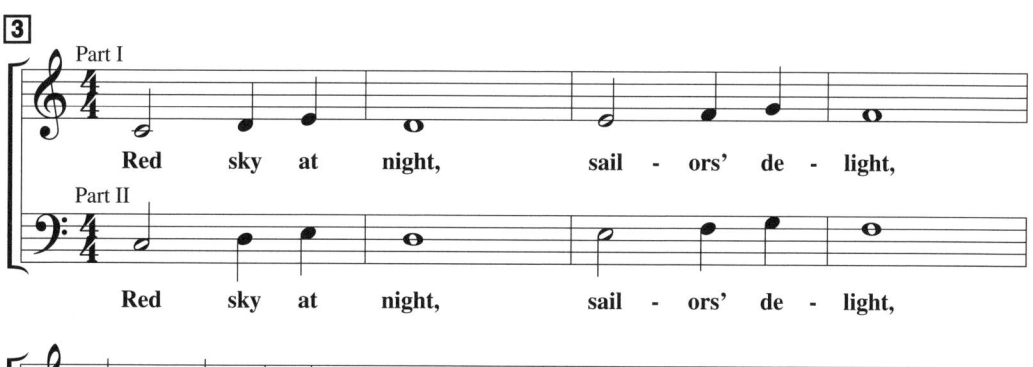

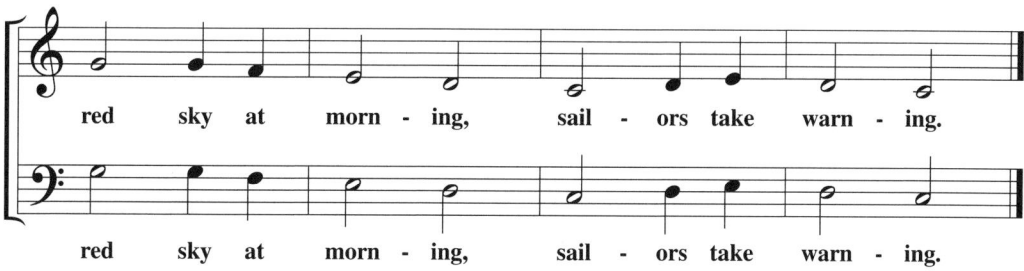

2.5 Sight-Read

CHAPTER 3

3.1 Whole Steps and Half Steps

Remember the *key* is the importance of one pitch over the others in a scale. The keynote is described as the home tone. The *key of C* played on the piano would begin on C and progress stepwise using only the white keys of the piano.

These steps on the piano for the key of C are an arrangement of whole steps and half steps.

- A *half step* is the smallest distance (or interval) between two notes on a keyboard.
- A *whole step* is the combination of two half steps side by side.
- A *major scale* is a specific arrangement of whole steps and half steps in the following order:

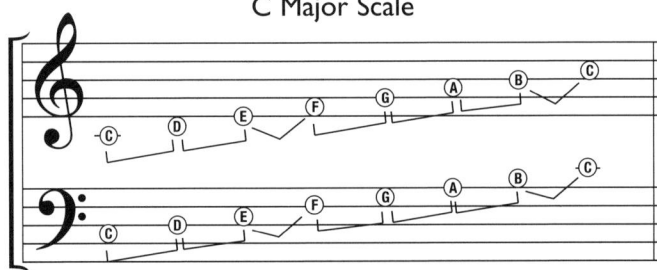

14   Essential Sight-Singing

3.2 Pitch Builder

Sing each line separately and in any combination.

3.3 Pitch Builder

Sing each line separately and in any combination.

3.4 Sight-Read

Winter
for SATB, a cappella

TENNYSON (Adapted)

Music by
EMILY CROCKER

CHAPTER 4

4.1 Sharps and Flats

You'll recall the order of whole and half steps for the C major scale:

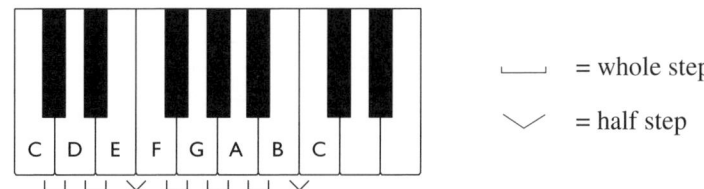

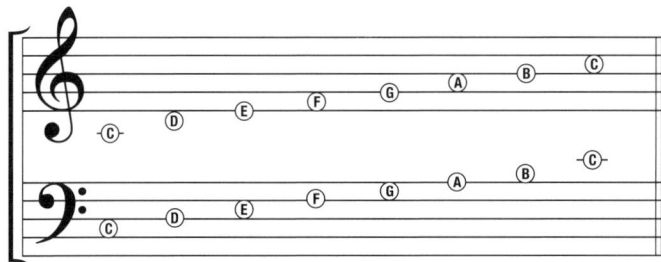

Music may be written with any note being the keynote. Because the order of whole steps and half steps must always be followed regardless of the keynote, the need arises for *sharps* (♯) and *flats* (♭).

A *sharp* raises the pitch one half step. These notes, F♯ (F sharp), would be written with the sharp sign to the left of the noteheads.

A *flat* lowers the pitch one half step. These notes, B♭ (B flat), would be written with the flat sign to the left of the noteheads.

4.2 Key of G Major

To build a major scale starting on G, using the same arrangement of whole steps and half steps as in the key of C major, you'll notice the need for an F♯.

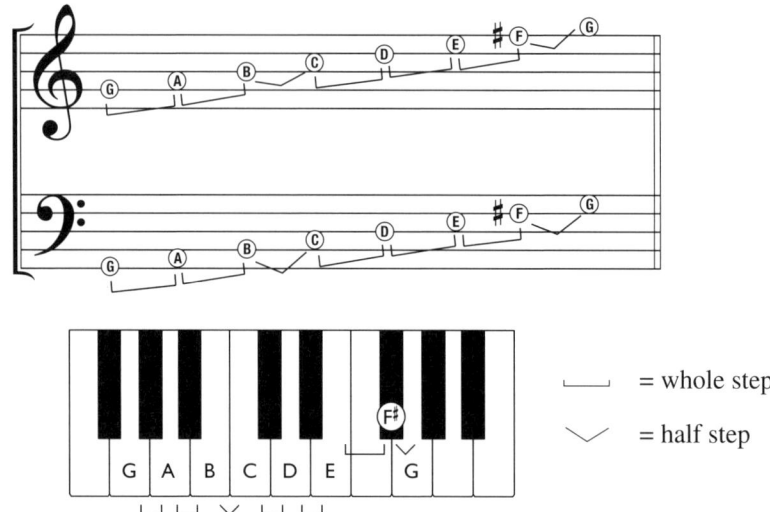

If we had written F - G, the *interval* (distance) between these two pitches would have been a whole step rather than the required half step.

Key of G Practice

Practice singing the G major scale. In each clef, two octaves of this scale are written below. Because of the wider range, you may only be able to sing a portion of the two octaves, but take note of your own vocal range. What is your lowest note? Your highest note?

Remember that middle C can be written on its own little line in either clef. Other pitches may be written that way also. These little lines are called *ledger lines.* Ledger lines may be used to represent notes either above or below the staff.

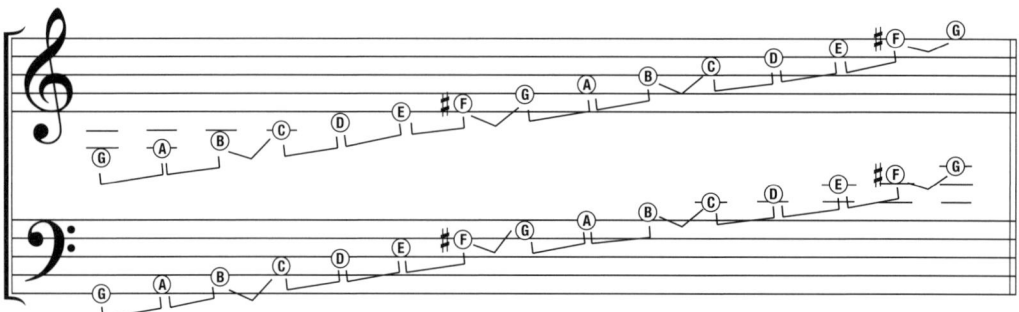

4.3 Pitch Builder

Identify the following pitches in the key of G major. Echo sing or sing as a group.

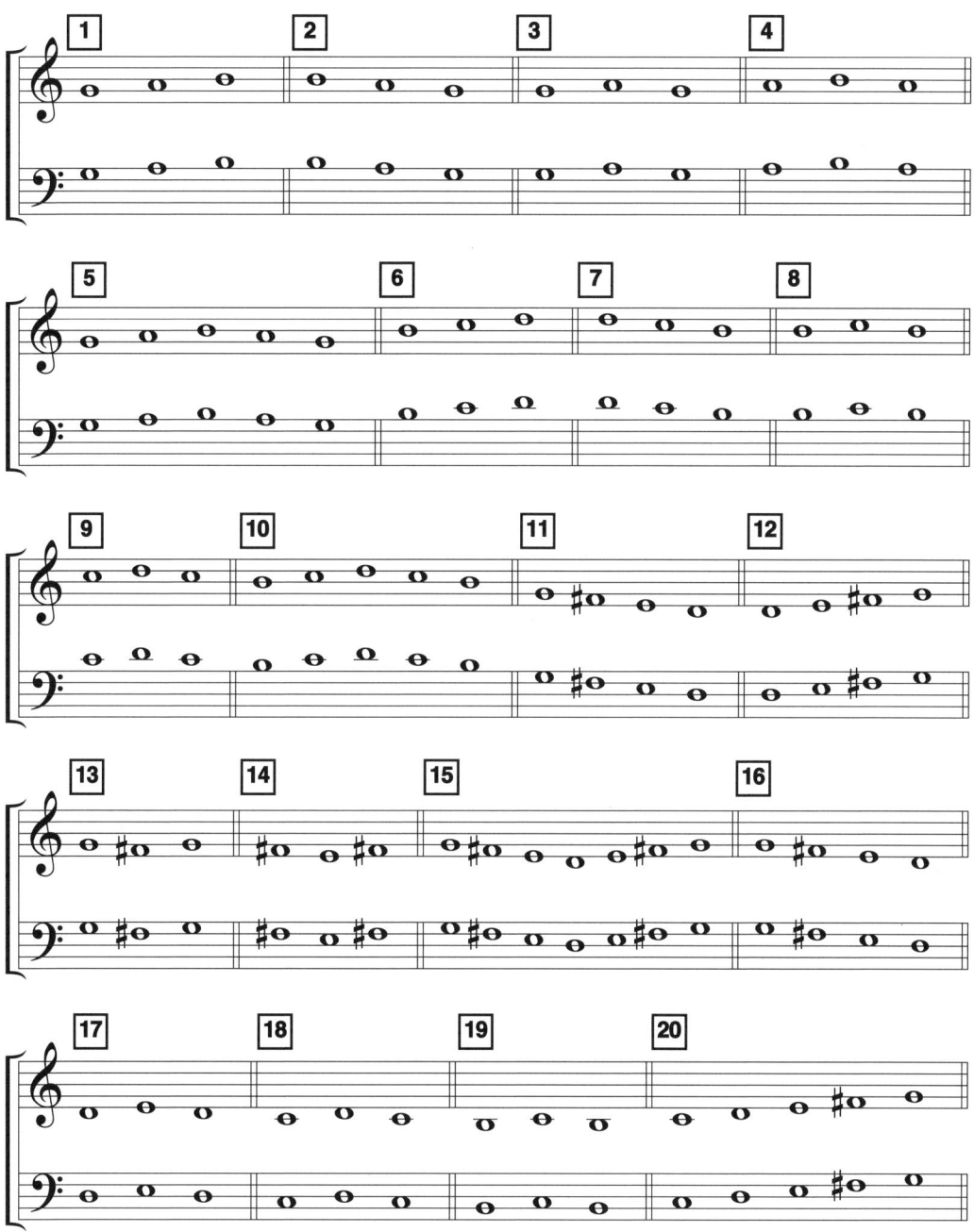

4.4 Pitch Builder

Sing each line separately and in any combination.

4.5 Sight-Read

Sing Your Songs
Tr. #9

for SATB, a cappella

Words and Music by
JOHN LEAVITT

p
calms all woe, soft - ly the
p
calms all woe, soft - ly the
p
calms all woe, soft - ly the
p
calms all woe, soft - ly the
p
7

mu - sic play - ing.
mu - sic play - ing.
mu - sic play - ing.
mu - sic play - ing.
10

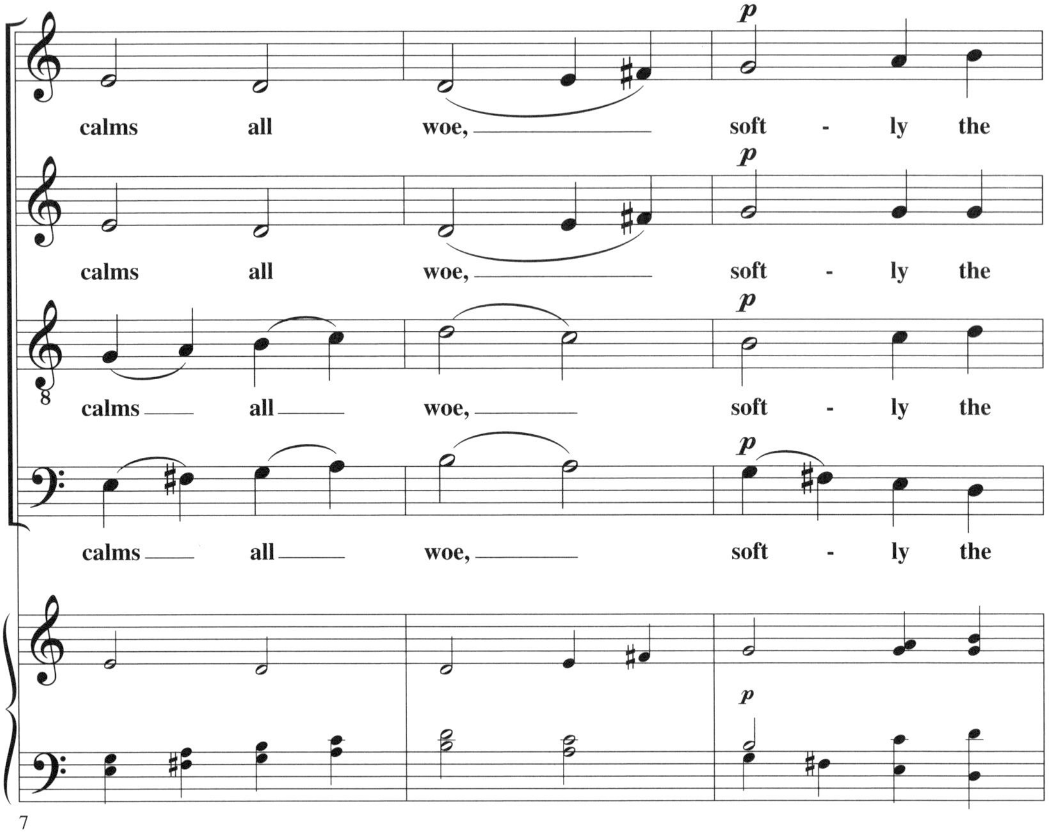

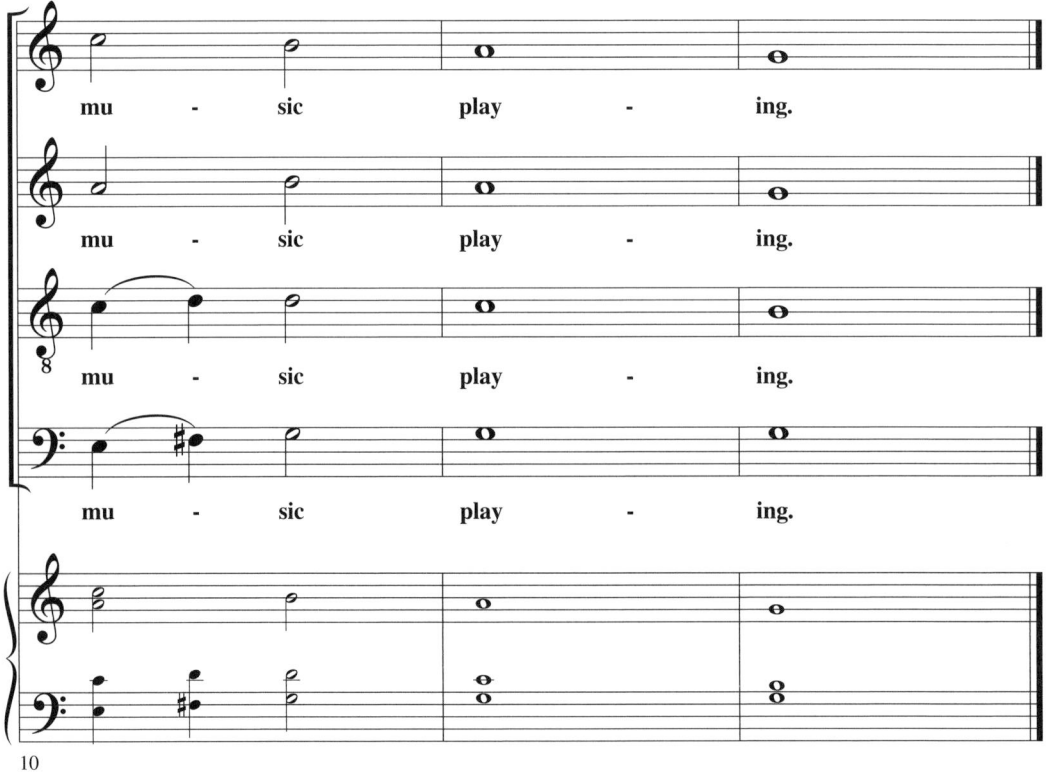

CHAPTER 5

5.1 Accidentals and Key Signature

A *sharp* raises the pitch one half step. These notes, F♯ (F sharp), would be written with the sharp sign to the left of the noteheads.

A *flat* lowers the pitch one half step. These notes, B♭ (B flat), would be written with the flat sign to the left of the noteheads.

There are two ways to write sharps and flats in music. One way is to write the sharp or flat to the left of the noteheads as shown above. These are called *accidentals* because they are not normally found in the key in which you are performing.

The other way is to write a *key signature*. Since we know that the key of G major will always use an F♯, rather than write the sharp sign on every F in the song, we simply write a sharp on F's line at the beginning of the song right after the clef sign(s) and before the time signature. (Note: The key signature is used with every clef sign in the song as a reminder).

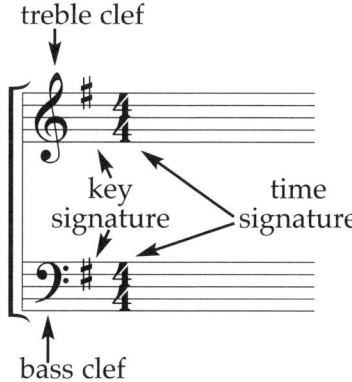

Placing an F♯ in the key signature indicates that the music is in the key of *G major* which always uses an F♯. Remember that the key of *C major* has no sharps or flats. Thus, the absence of sharps or flats in the key signature indicates that the music is in the key of C major.

5.2 Pitch Builder

Sing each line separately and in any combination. Notice that not every melody starts on the keynote G. Identify the starting pitch of each melody and sing up or down the scale to locate the starting pitch.

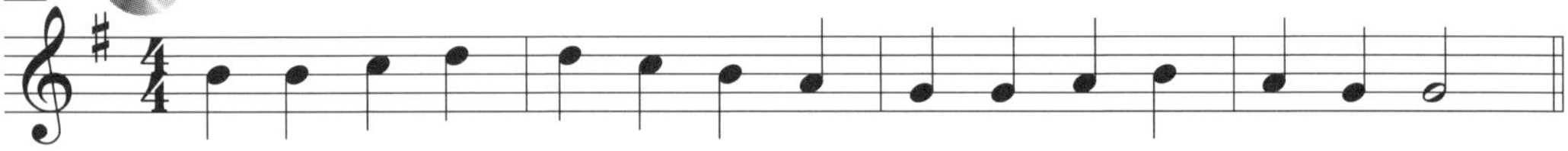

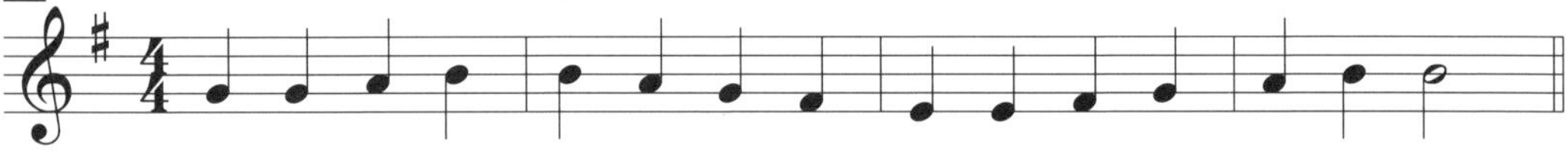

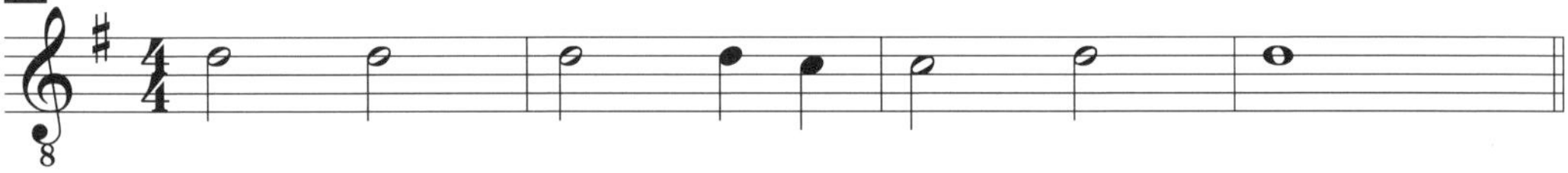

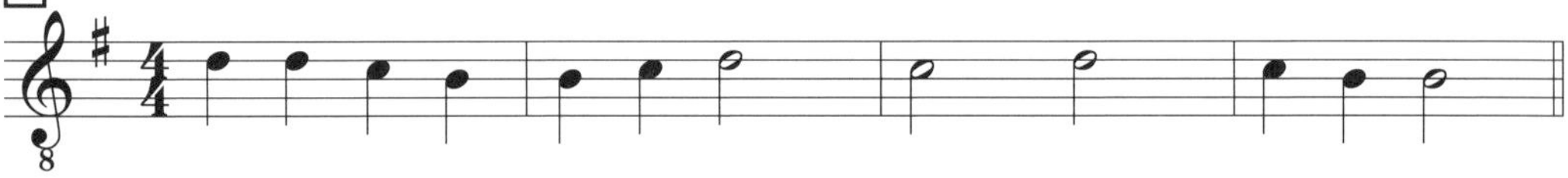

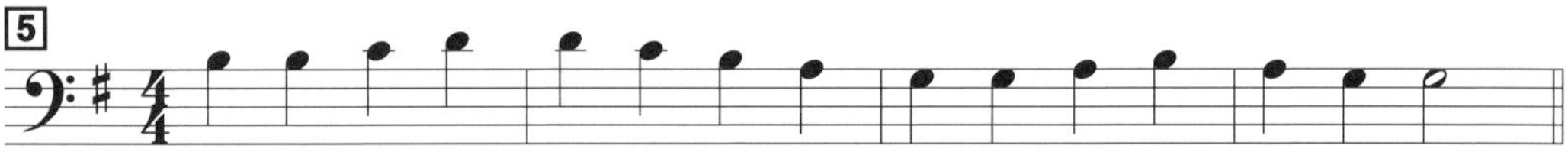

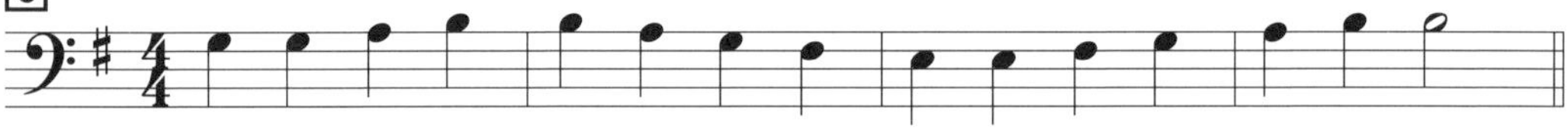

1 Tr. #10

2

3

4

5

6

5.3 Sight-Read

Tr. #11 Joyfully Sing

for 3-Part Mixed, a cappella

Words and Music by
EMILY CROCKER

Joyfully (♩ = *ca.* 168)

Part I
Part II
Part III

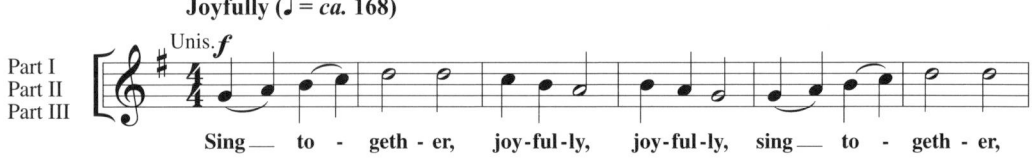

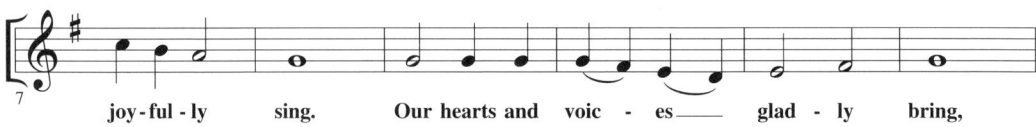

*Accompaniment CD plays m. 25-32 a total of 3 times.

5.4 Rests

Rests are silences in music. They come in a variety of lengths, just like notes. These silences are just as important as the notes.

	notes	rests
whole	𝅝	𝄻
half	𝅗𝅥	𝄼
quarter	♩	𝄽

Rests and notes of the same name share the same duration.

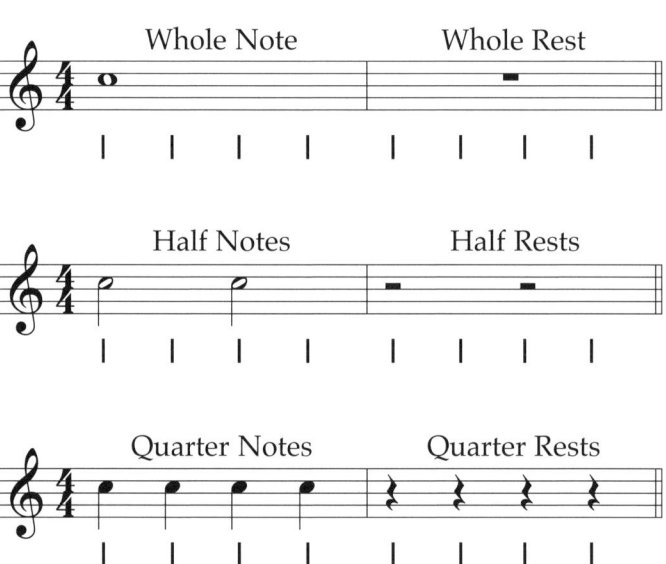

5.5 Rhythm Builder

Read each line (clap, tap, or chant).

5.6 Sight-Read

Tr. #12 Animal Song

for 4-Part Speech Chorus

Divide the choir into any number of groups up to four. Each group may chant one of the four numbered parts. Each part may proceed to the next part sequentially without a break in rhythm (eg. Group 1 sings parts 1-2-3-4, Group 2 sings parts 2-3-4-1, etc.). Work for a sing-song kind of inflected speech at a light dynamic level. Practice slowly at first and gradually increase the speed of the beat. Note: Accompaniment CD plays song four times.

Traditional Lyrics

Music by
JOHN LEAVITT

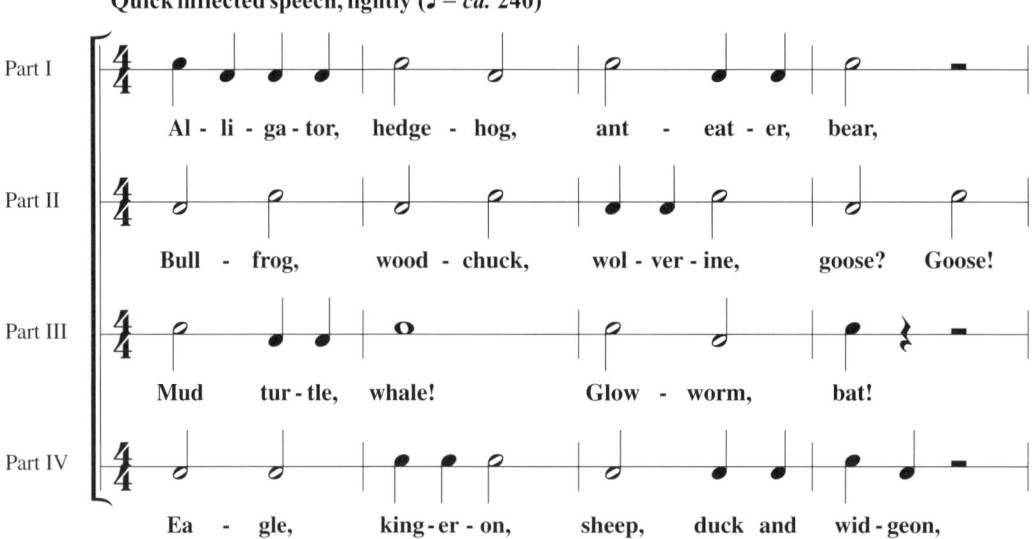

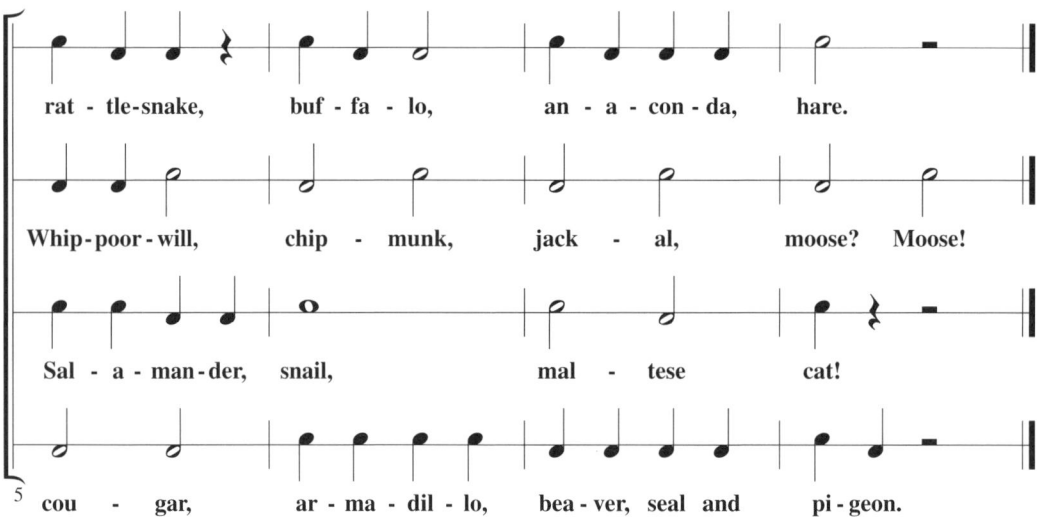

5.7 Pitch Builder

Sing each line separately and in any combination.

5.8 Sight-Read

 Rain

for 2-Part Mixed and Piano

The text for this short piece was written by the Scottish poet Robert Louis Stevenson and included in his collection of poems for children: *A Child's Garden of Verses*. Stevenson, who lived from 1850-1894, also wrote two of the most famous novels ever written, *Treasure Island* and *The Strange Case of Dr. Jekyll and Mr. Hyde*.

Words by
ROBERT LOUIS STEVENSON

Music by
EMILY CROCKER

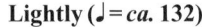

CHAPTER 6

6.1 Melodic Intervals

An *interval* is the measurement of distance between two pitches. When intervals are played in succession, they are called *melodic intervals*. Following are examples of intervals of 2nds, 3rds, 4ths, and 5ths.

Read the pitches, echo sing, or sing each example as a group:

6.2 Pitch Builder

Practice the following exercises. Echo sing or sing as a group.

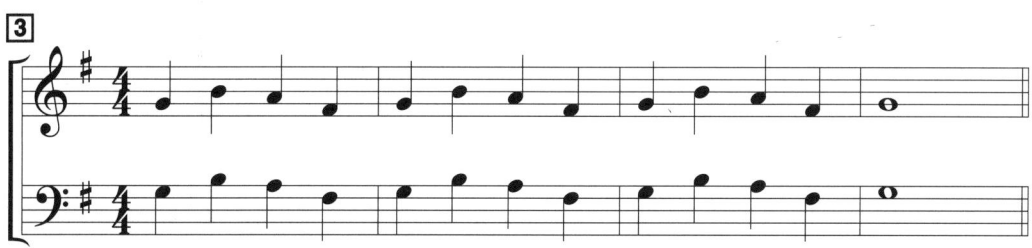

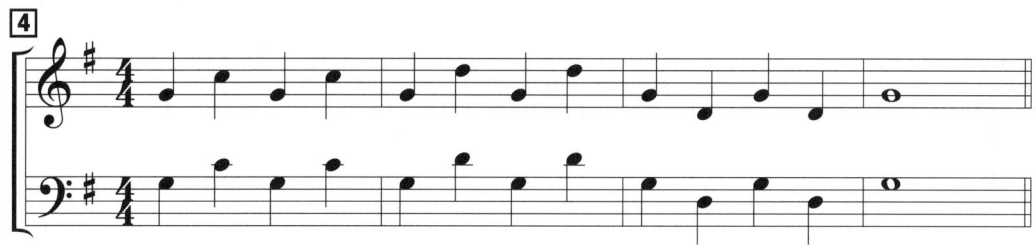

6.3 Sight-Read

Sing Hosanna

for SATB, a cappella

Traditional

Music by
JOHN LEAVITT

6.4 Harmonic Intervals

To review, an *interval* is the measurement between two pitches. When intervals are played in succession, they are called *melodic intervals*.

When intervals are played simultaneously, they are called *harmonic intervals*. Here are some examples of harmonic intervals.

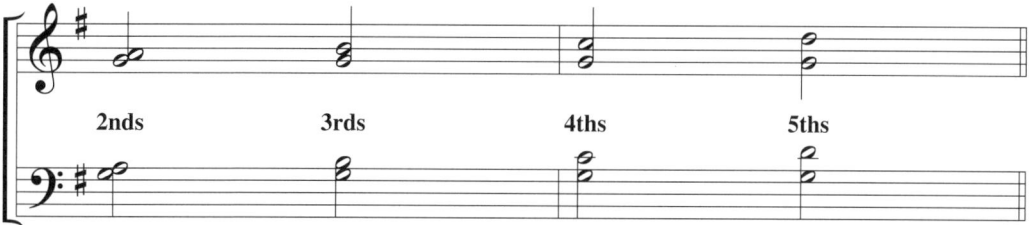

Harmonic intervals are the building blocks of harmony. Two or more harmonic intervals combined form a chord. Thus, a *chord* is the combination of three or more tones played simultaneously. Here are some examples of chords.

6.5 Pitch Builder

Practice the following exercises. Notice the harmonic intervals that result when one part sustains a pitch while the other part moves to a higher or lower pitch. Listen carefully for balance, tuning, and blend.

Practice the following exercises in three parts. Notice the chord that results as one part sustains a pitch while the other parts move higher and lower.

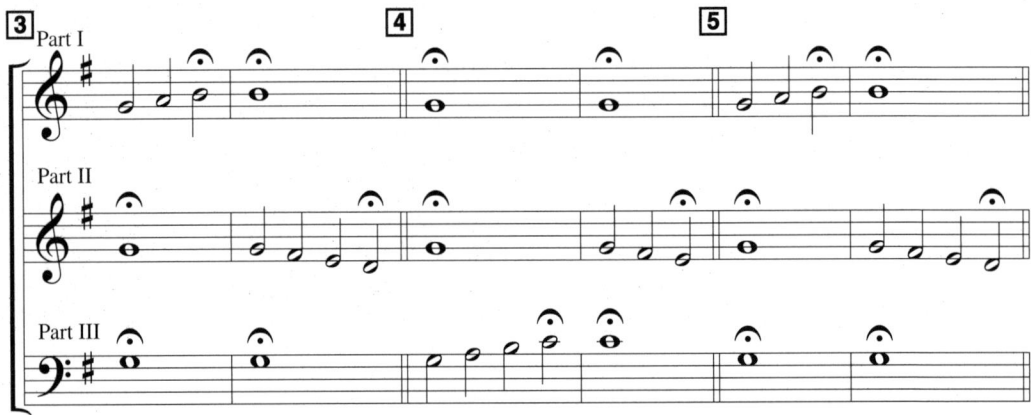

6.6 Pitch Builder

Sing each line separately and in any combination.

6.7 Sight-Read

for SATB and Piano

The author of this text, *Francis Beaumont,* was an English playwright who lived from c. 1584-1616 and was a contemporary of William Shakespeare. It was quite common for plays of this period to use music.

Text by
FRANCIS BEAUMONT

Music by
EMILY CROCKER

40 Essential Sight-Singing

CHAPTER 7

7.1 Tonic Chord

Two or more harmonic intervals combined form a chord. A *chord* is the combination of three or more tones played or sung simultaneously.

A *triad* is a special type of three-note chord built in thirds over a *root tone*. Following are some examples of triads.

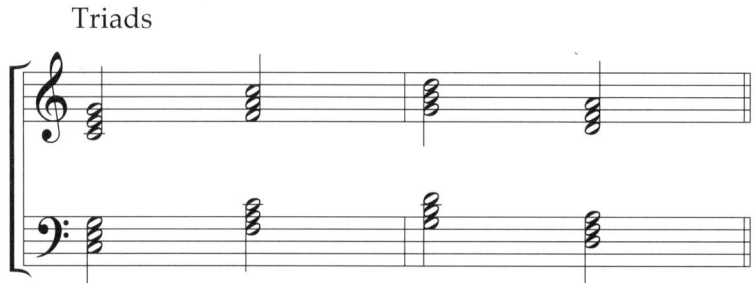

When a *triad* is built on the keynote of a major scale it is called a *tonic chord*. You'll notice that the word *tonic* is related to the word "tone." Tonic is another way of referring to the keynote of a major scale, and *tonic chord* is another way of referring to the triad built on that keynote.

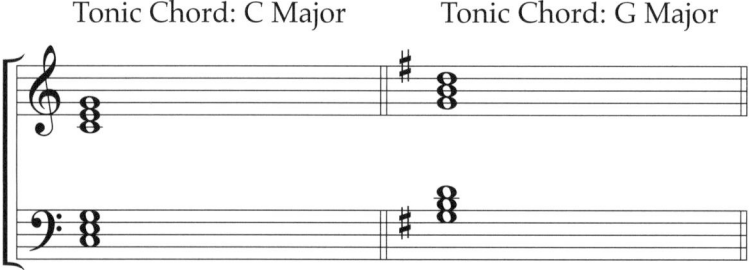

7.2 Pitch Builder

Practice the following drills which outline the tonic chord. Remember, when the melody outlines the tonic chord, you are singing melodic intervals. When three or more parts sing the pitches of the tonic chord simultaneously, the ensemble is singing a chord.

Tonic Drill

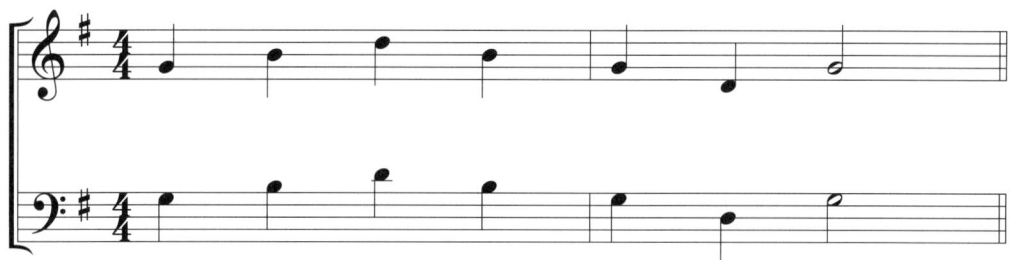

Melody Drill

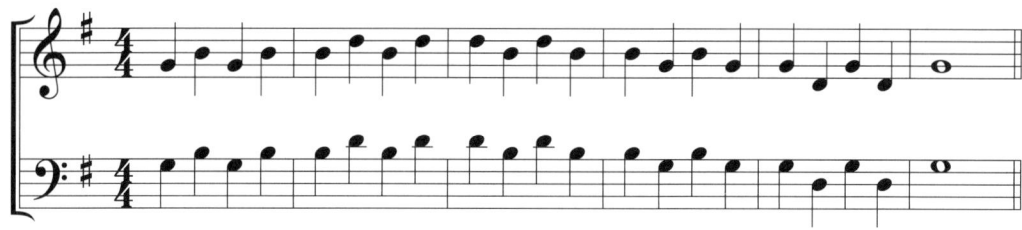

Chord Builders

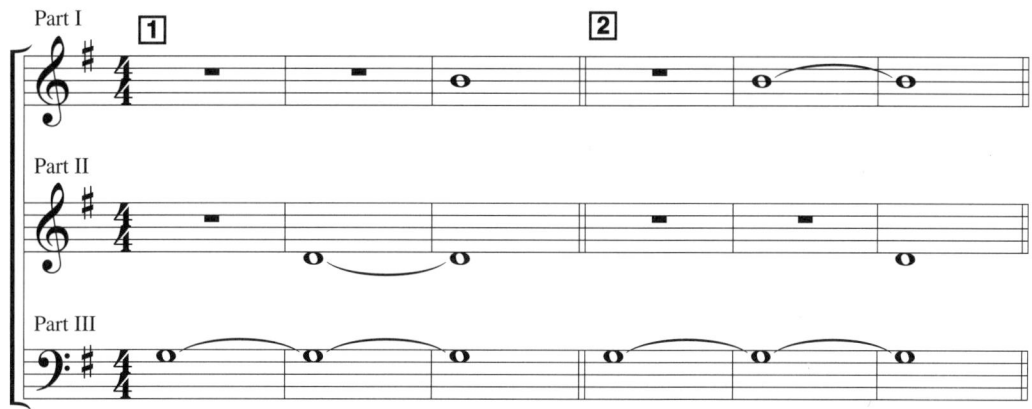

7.3 Pitch Builder

Sing each line separately and in any combination.

7.4 Sight-Read
O Music, Sweet Music

for 3-Part Mixed, a cappella

Words by
LOWELL MASON

Music by
JOHN LEAVITT

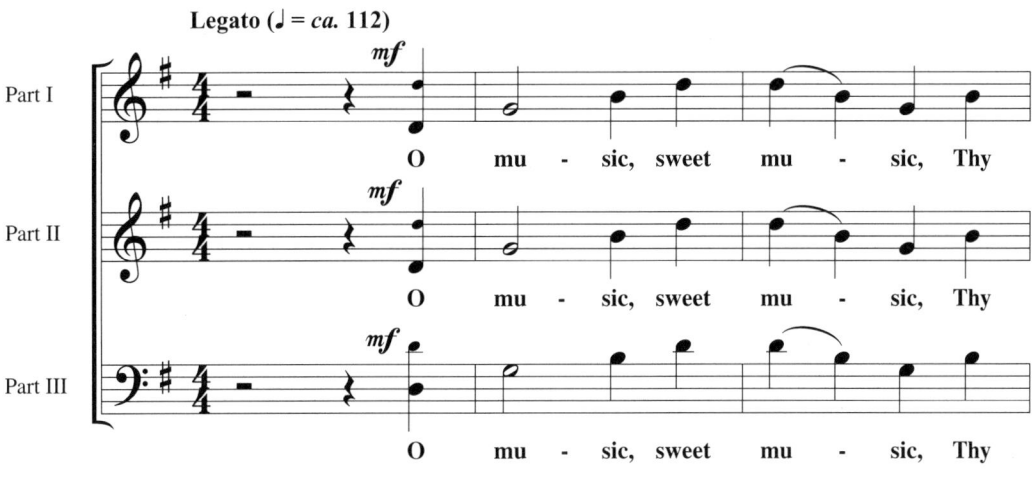

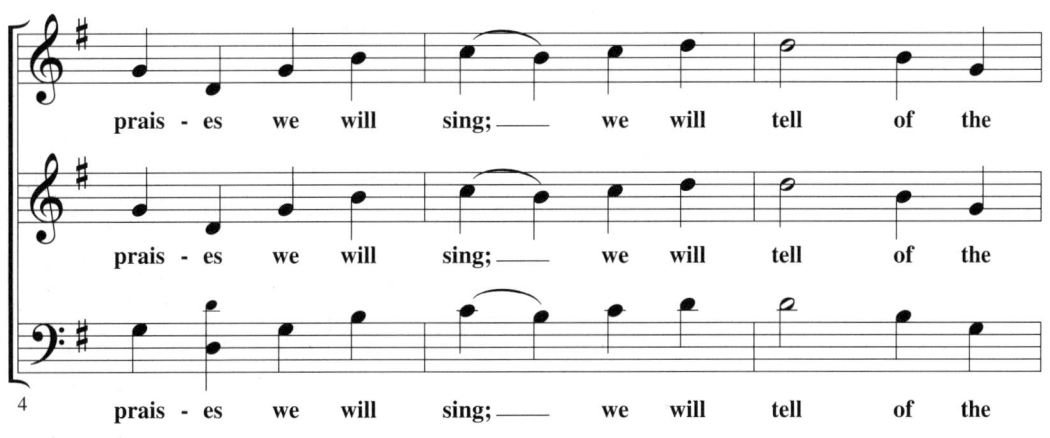

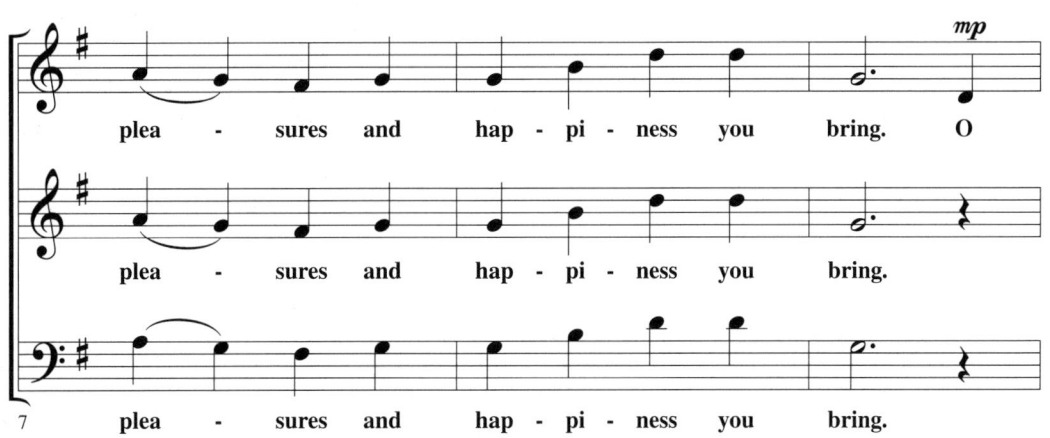

*Accompaniment CD provides 3 beats of clicks before music begins.

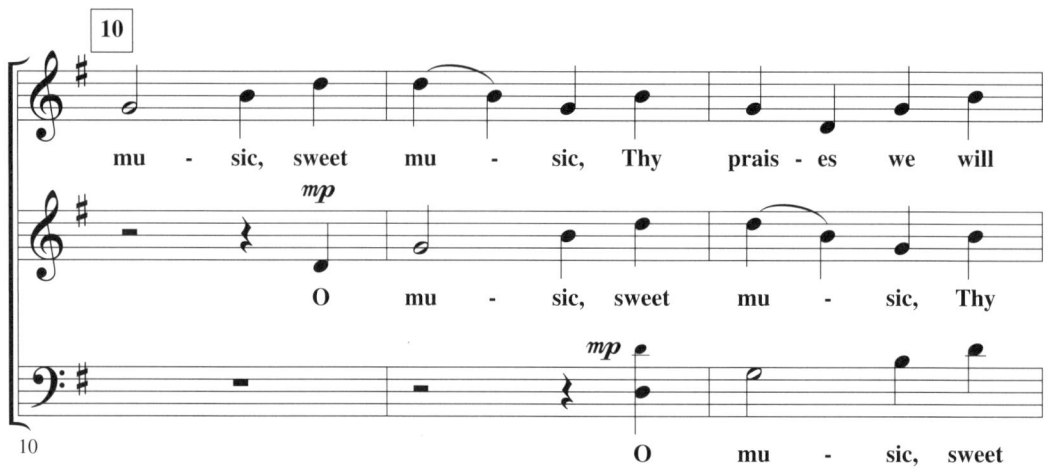
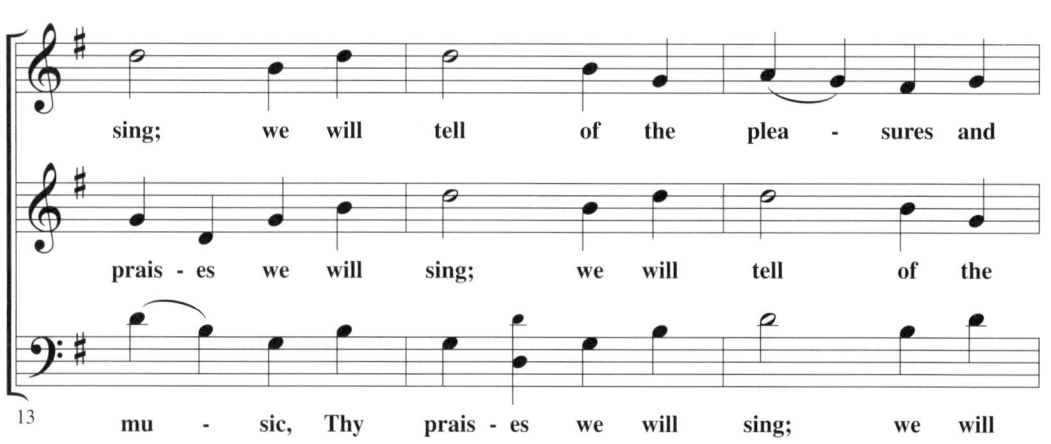
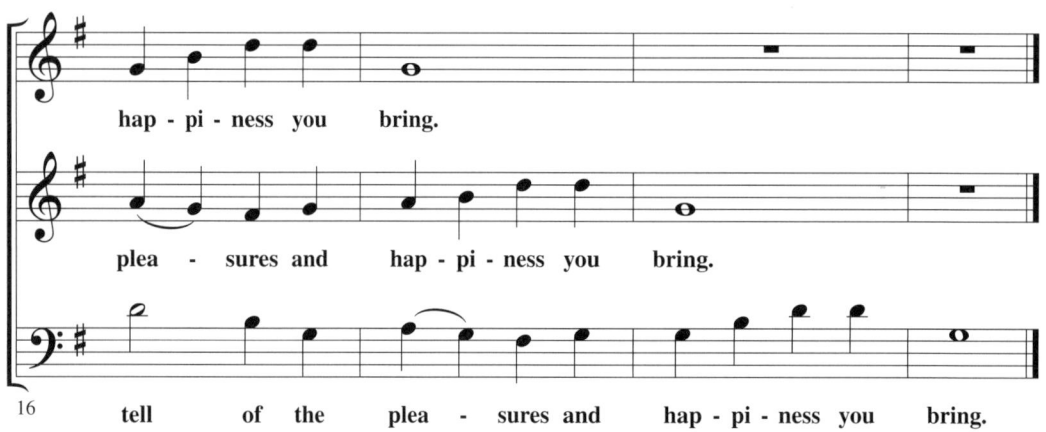

48 Essential Sight-Singing

7.5 Pitch Builder

Pickup notes (also called *upbeat* or *anacrusis*) are one or more notes which occur before the first barline.

Sing each line separately and in any combination. Notice the *pickup note* in each exercise.*

*Accompaniment CD provides 3 beats of clicks before music begins.

7.6 Sight-Read

Hosanna
for SATB and Piano

Music by
JOHN LEAVITT

8.1 Key of F Major

The key of F major indicates that the keynote will be F. The staff below shows the F major scale as well as the whole/half step progression that is required for a major scale.

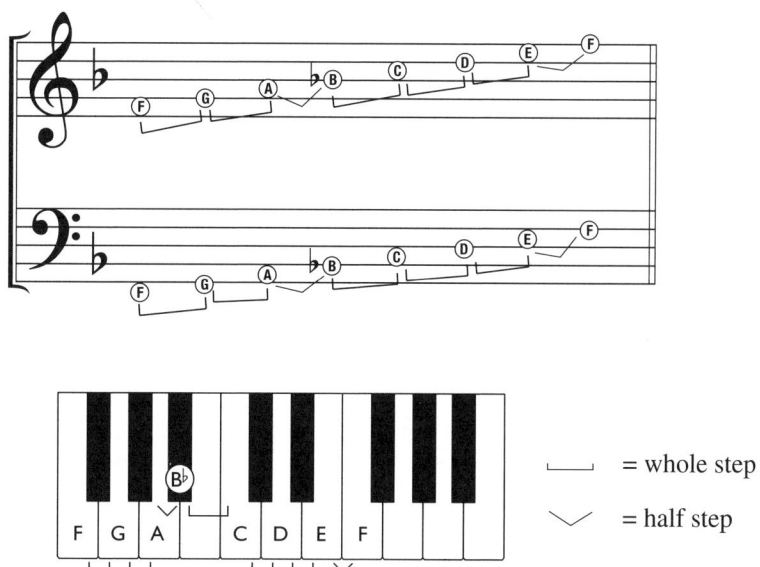

In F major, the whole/half step progression requires a B♭. (Remember that a flat lowers a pitch by one half step.) If we had written A-B, the interval between these two pitches would have been a whole step rather than the required half step.

Remember also that a key signature is placed after the clef sign at the beginning of a line. This time the flat is on B's line, and it indicates that every time B occurs in the music, it should be sung as a B♭.

Dotted Notes

In music notation, we need to be able to measure note values with durations of three beats (especially in meters of 3). Our notational system accomplishes this by adding a dot to the right of a notehead. The rule governing dotted notes is the dot receives *half the value of the note to which it is attached.*

8.2 Pitch Builder

Practice the following drills which outline the tonic chord. Remember, when the melody outlines the tonic chord, you are singing melodic intervals. When three or more parts sing pitches simultaneously, the ensemble is singing a chord.

8.3 Pitch Builder

Exercises in 4/4
Sing each line separately and in any combination.

Exercises in 3/4
Sing each line separately and in any combination.

8.4 Sight-Read

The Call
for SATB, a cappella

Words by
GEORGE HERBERT (1593-1633)

Music by
JOHN LEAVITT

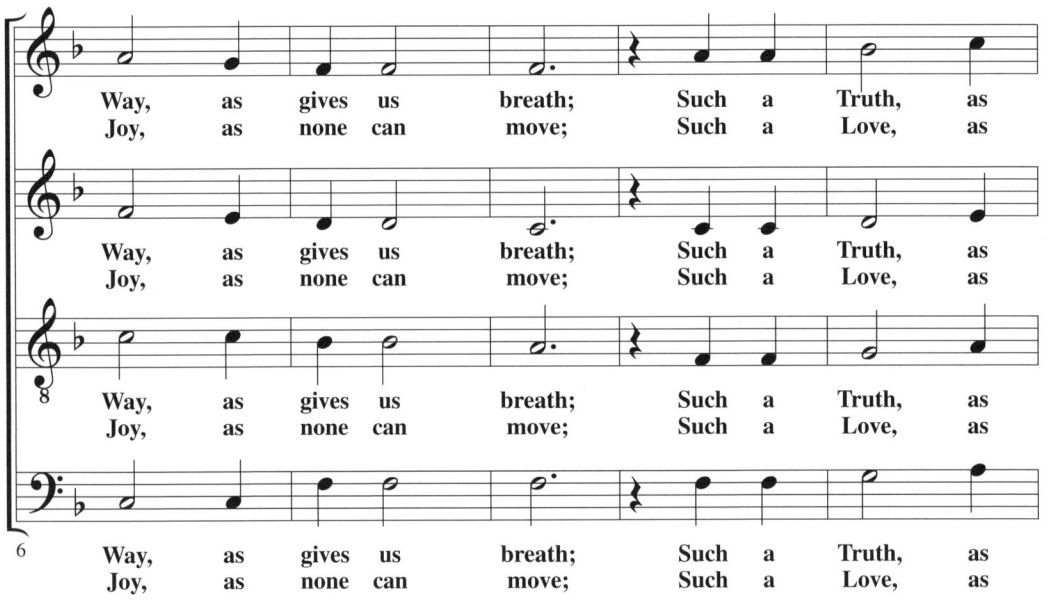

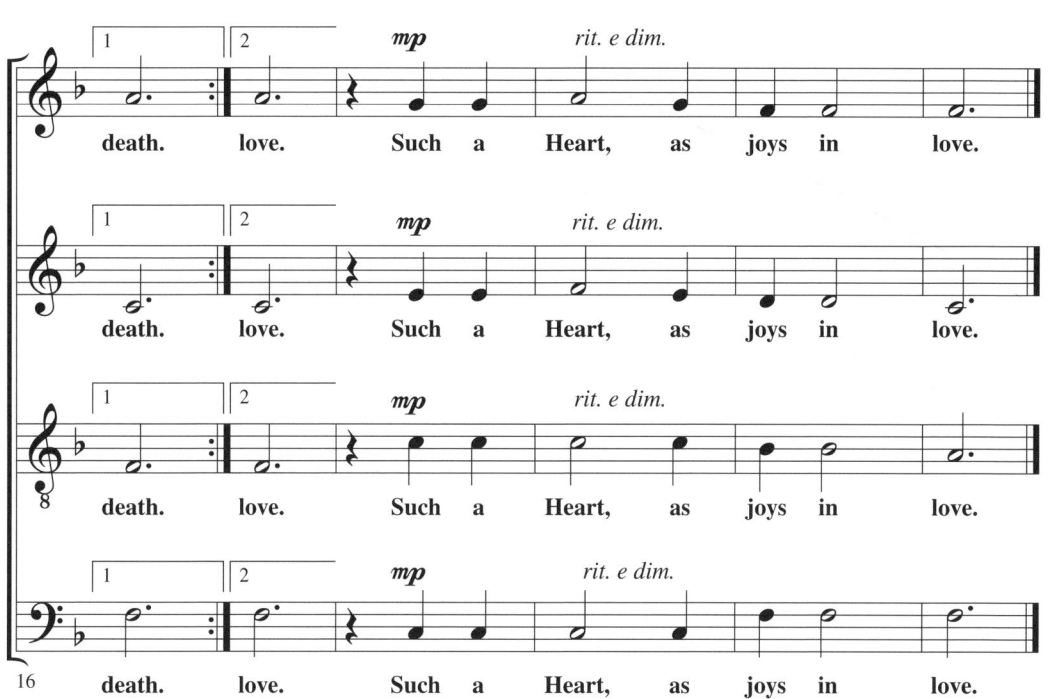

CHAPTER 9

9.1 Eighth Notes and Rests

So far, we've used whole, half, and quarter notes. An *eighth note* (♪) is half the value of a quarter note. Two eighth notes (♫) have the same duration as one quarter note. The eighth note has a corresponding rest, the eighth rest (𝄾), which shares the same length as an eighth note.

Below is a chart summarizing the notes and rests we've learned.

	notes	rests
whole	𝅝	𝄻
half	𝅗𝅥	𝄼
quarter	♩	𝄽
eighth	♪	𝄾

The following diagram summarizes the relationships between the notes we've studied:

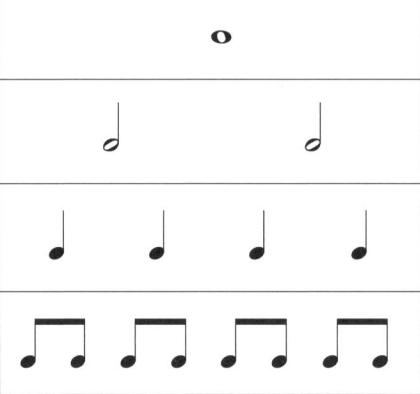

If the quarter note receives the beat, you can consider eighth notes to be a division of the beat:

Beat: ♩ ♩ ♩ ♩

Division: ♫ ♫ ♫ ♫

Eighth notes may be notated singly with a stem and a flag:

♪ ♪ ♪ ♪

Or they may be beamed together in groups:

58   Essential Sight-Singing

9.2 Rhythm Builder

Read each line (clap, tap, or chant).

9.3 Rhythm Builder

Read each line (clap, tap, or chant).

9.4 Sight-Read

Tr. #25 Hey Diddle Diddle!
for 2-Part Speech Chorus

Hey Diddle Diddle! is an English nursery rhyme. Sometimes these rhymes are called "Mother Goose" rhymes, but no one knows exactly why. We don't know who made them up or when they began. Rhymes for little children like this one exist in many different languages and cultures around the world.

English Nursery Rhyme

Music by
EMILY CROCKER

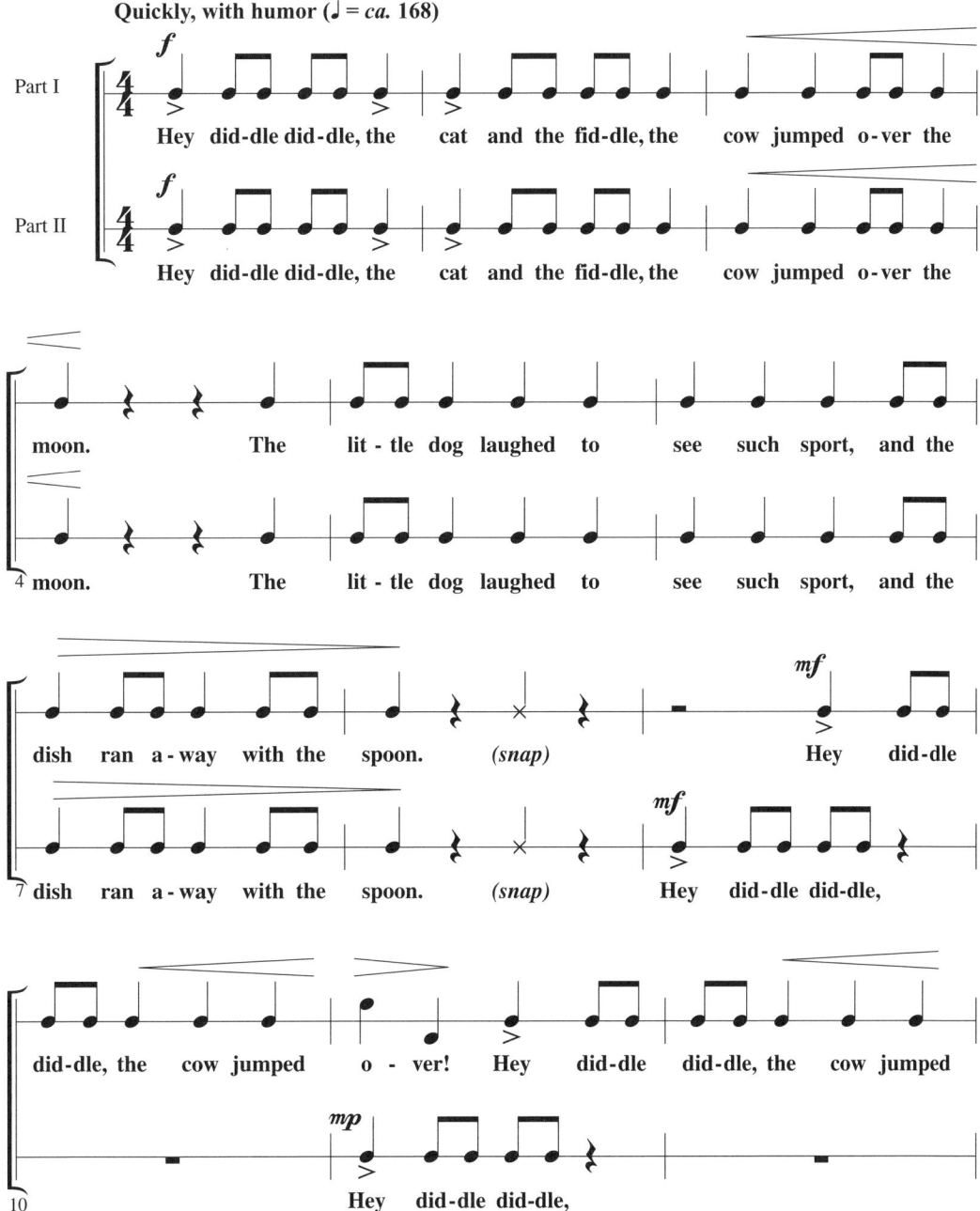

9.5 Pitch Builder

Sing each line separately and in any combination. Describe the time and key signatures.

9.6 Sight-Read

Betty Botter

for SATB, a cappella

Traditional Rhyme

Arranged by
JOHN LEAVITT

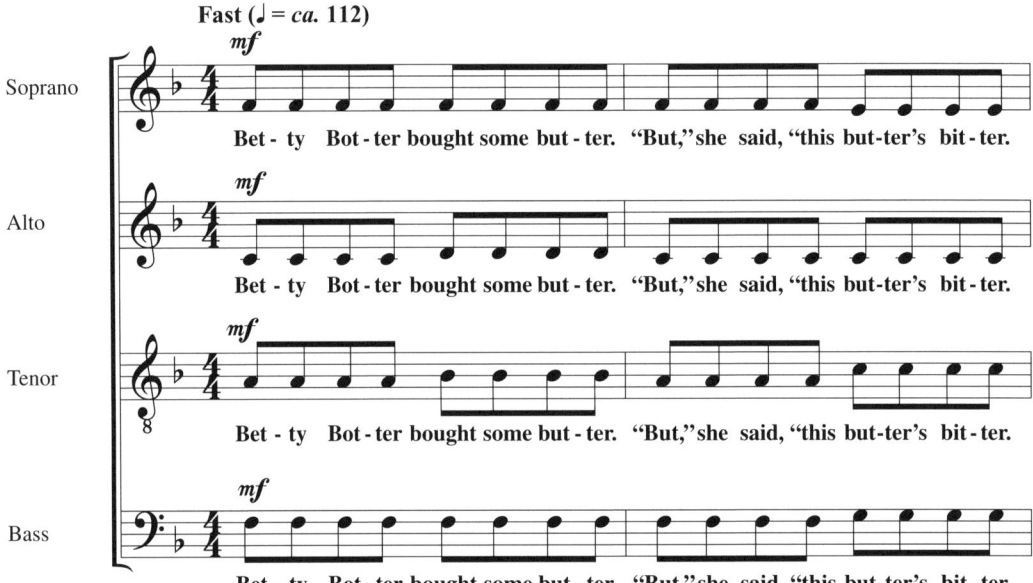

CHAPTER 10

10.1 Changing Meters

Remember that *meter* is a form of rhythmic organization. In the simple meters we have been using, the top number indicates the number of beats per measure in the music. The bottom number indicates which note value receives the beat.

4 = Four beats per measure (♩ ♩ ♩ ♩).
4 = The quarter note (♩) receives the beat.

3 = Three beats per measure (♩ ♩ ♩).
4 = The quarter note (♩) receives the beat.

2 = Two beats per measure (♩ ♩).
4 = The quarter note (♩) receives the beat.

So that the ear can easily recognize and group notes into the various meters, each meter stresses certain beats. Almost all meters stress the first beat of each measure. This is called the *downbeat*.

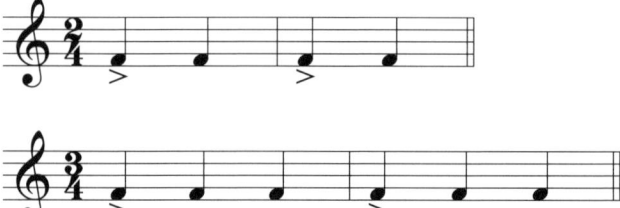

In 4/4 meter, a secondary stress occurs on beat three, along with the stressed downbeat.

10.2 Rhythm Builder
Read the following exercise with changing meters (clap, tap, or chant).

10.3 Sight-Read

 Alleluia

for SA, a cappella

Traditional Text

Music by JOHN LEAVITT

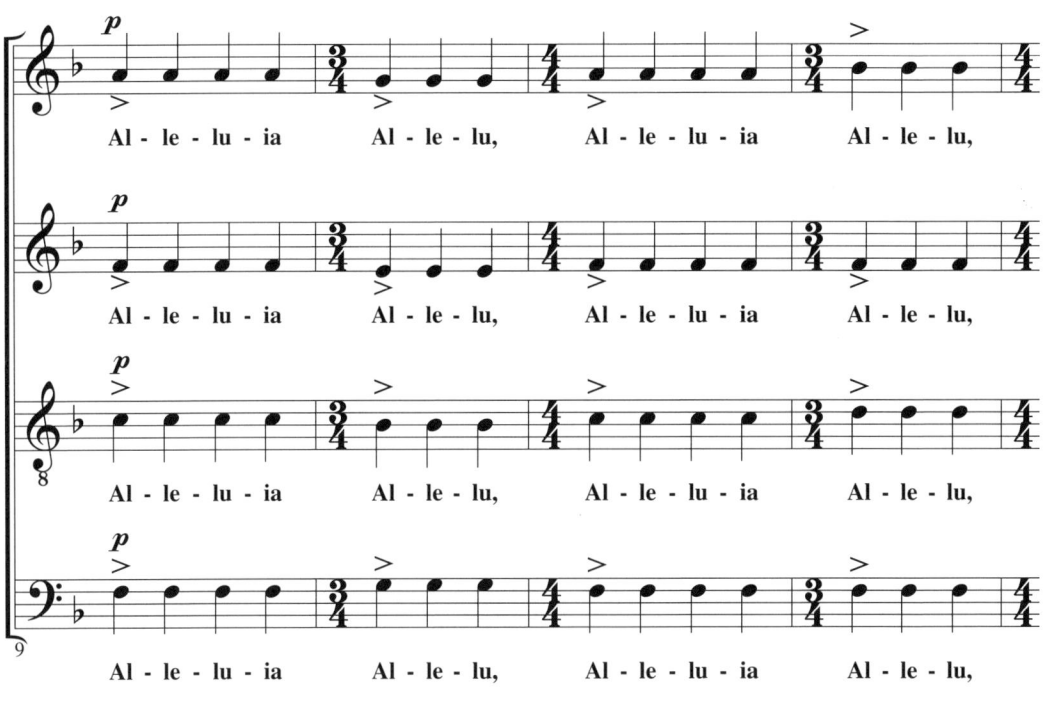

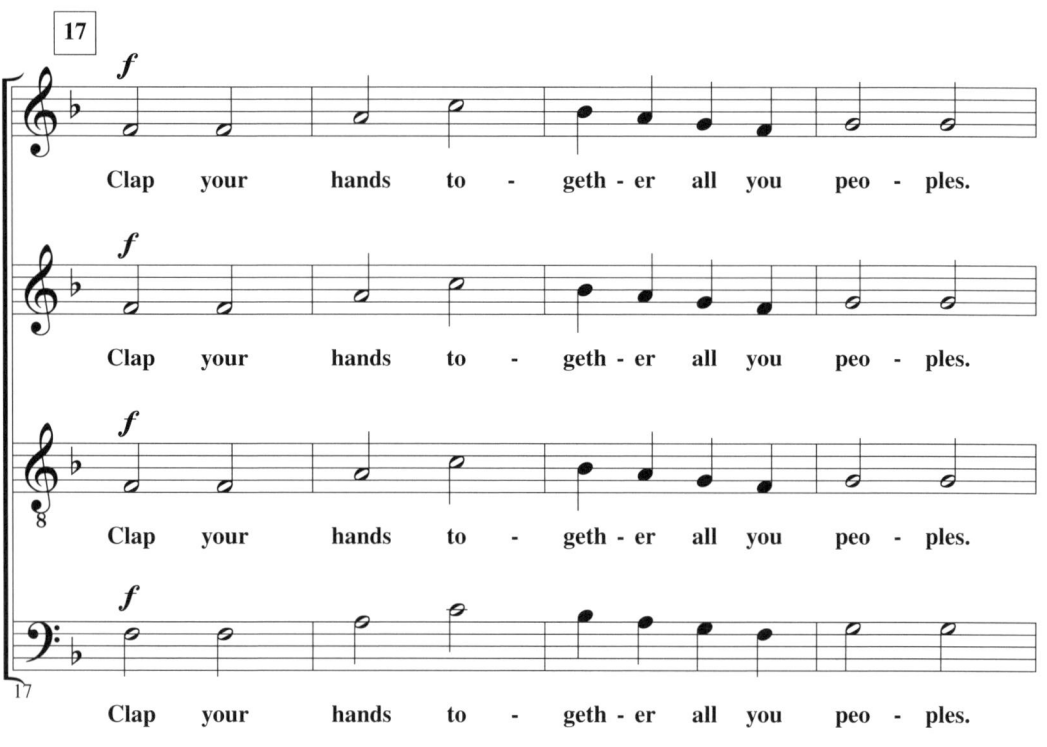

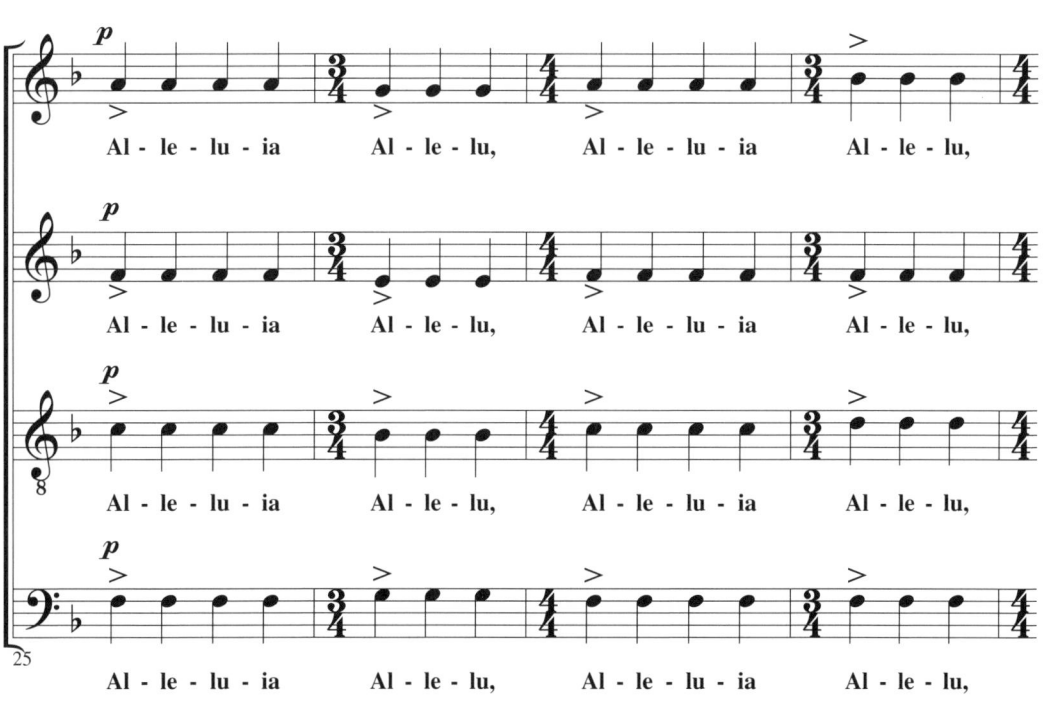

10.4 Sight-Read

The Bells
for SATB and Piano

Words by
EDGAR ALLEN POE

Music by
JOHN LEAVITT

APPENDIX

Solfège

Movable Do
"Do" changes as the key changes.

Key of C Major

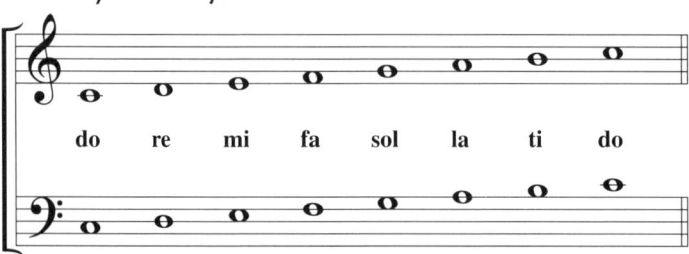

Key of G Major

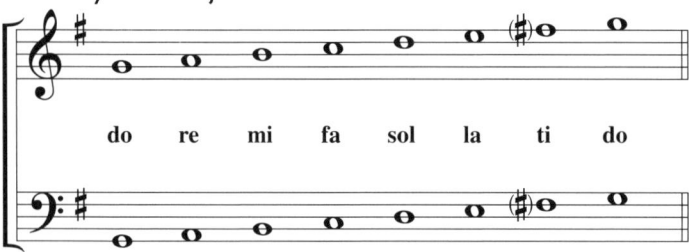

Accidentals change as the key changes.

Ascending Chromatics ("do" changes in each key)

Descending Chromatics ("do" changes in each key)

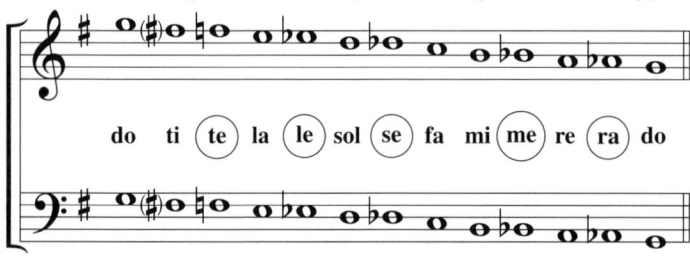

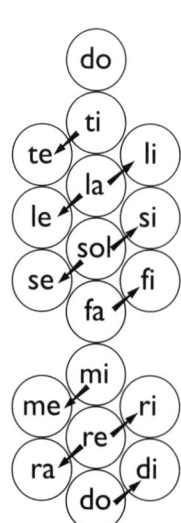

Solfège

Fixed Do
"Do" is C, and the pitch syllables remain fixed no matter what the key.

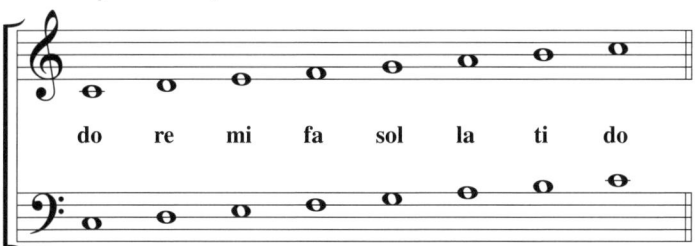

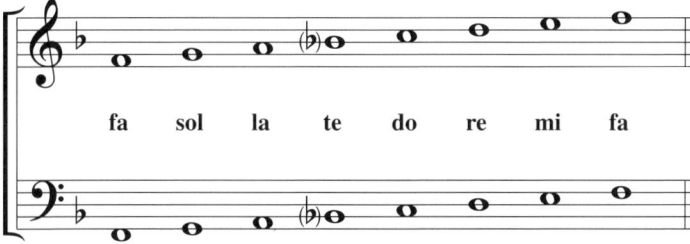

"Do" is C, and accidentals remain fixed no matter what the key.

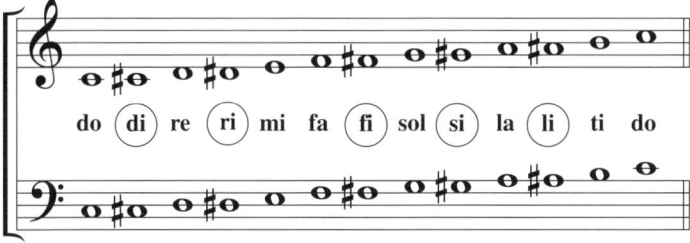

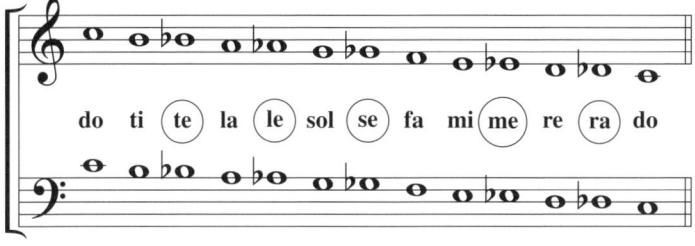

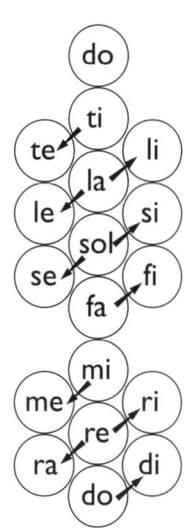

Numbers

Like movable "do," the "1" changes with each key.

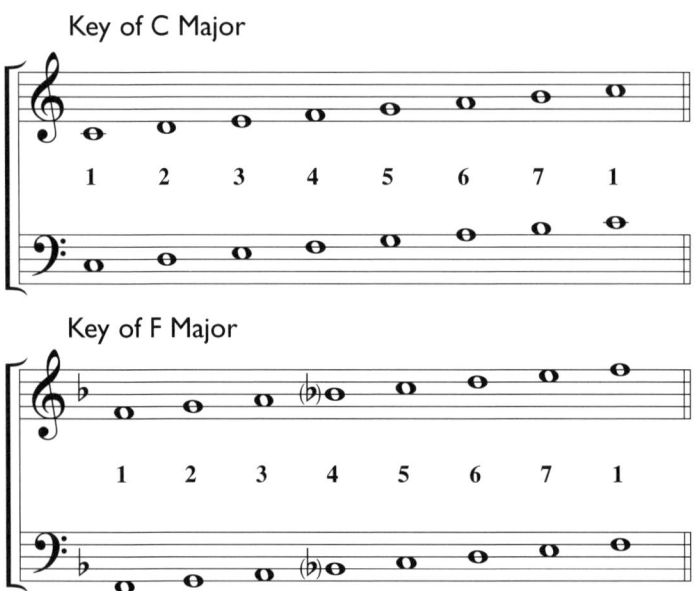

Accidentals can be performed either by singing the number but raising or lowering the pitch by a half step, or by singing the word "sharp" or "flat" before the number as a grace note.

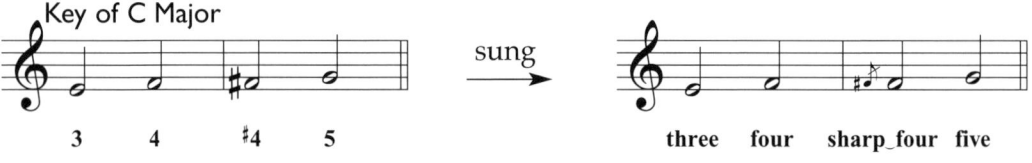

Counting Systems
The Kodály System

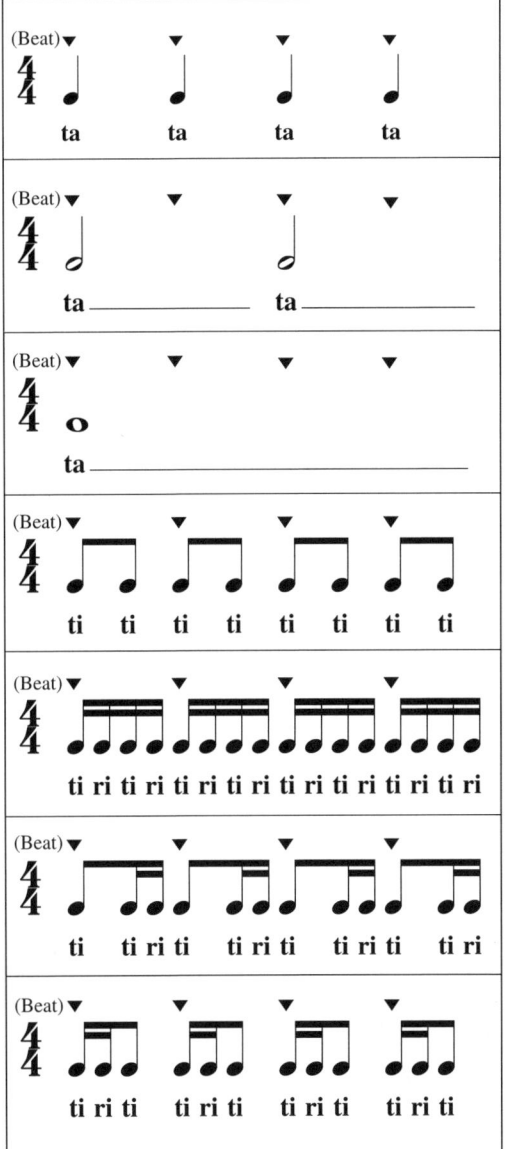
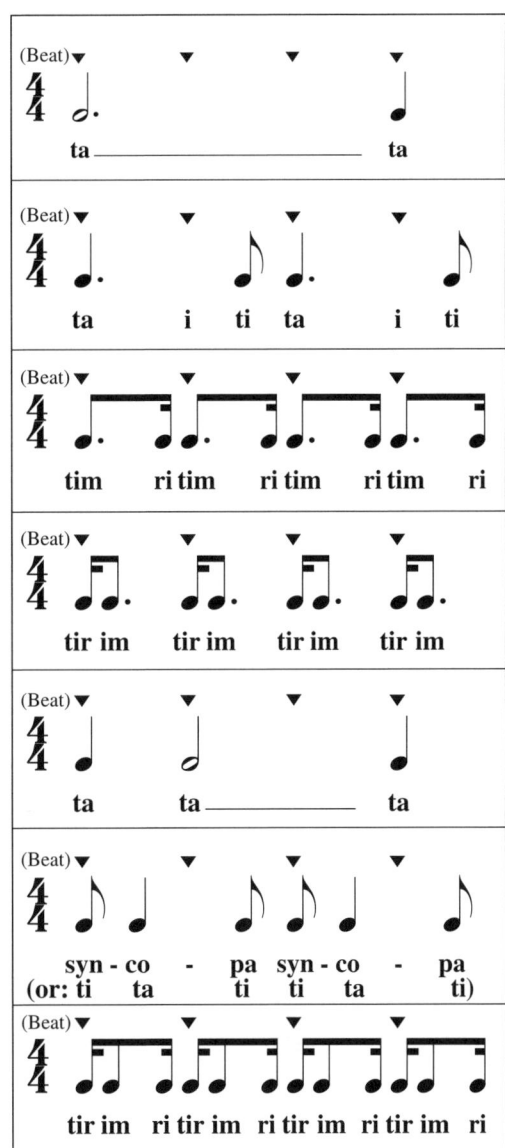
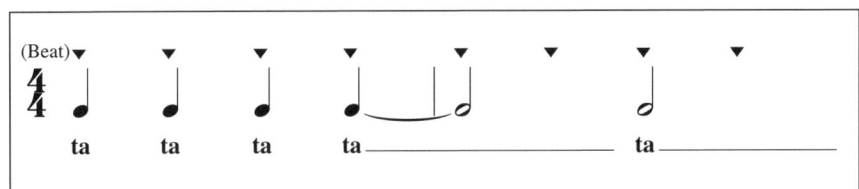

Counting Systems

The Traditional System

Counting Systems
The Eastman System

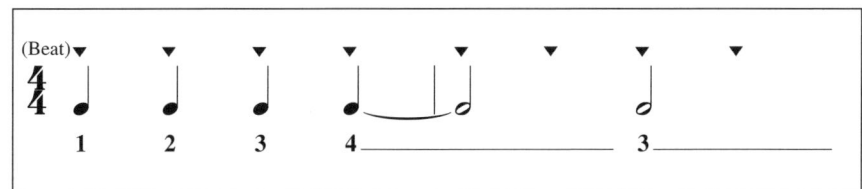

Other Simple Meters

Simple meters are based upon the note which receives the beat, i.e. $\frac{4}{4}$ meter is based upon the quarter note receiving the beat.

Adapt the information from the charts on pages 81-83 to apply to music in other simple meters:

2 = Two beats per measure (♪ ♪).
8 = The eighth note (♪) receives the beat.

3 = Three beats per measure (♪ ♪ ♪).
8 = The eighth note (♪) receives the beat.

4 = Four beats per measure (♪ ♪ ♪ ♪).
8 = The eighth note (♪) receives the beat.

2 = Two beats per measure (♩ ♩).
2 = The half note (♩) receives the beat. (Note: sometimes written as ¢ "cut time").

3 = Three beats per measure (♩ ♩ ♩).
2 = The half note (♩) receives the beat.

4 = Four beats per measure (♩ ♩ ♩ ♩).
2 = The half note (♩) receives the beat.

Compound Meter

Compound meters are meters which have a multiple of 3, such as 6 or 9 (but not 3 itself). Unlike simple meter which reflects the note that receives the beat, compound meter reflects the note that receives the division.

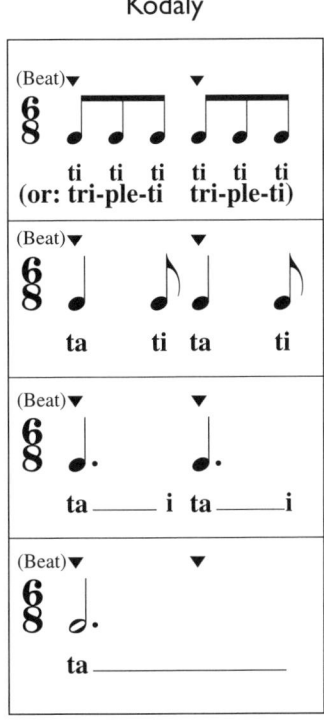
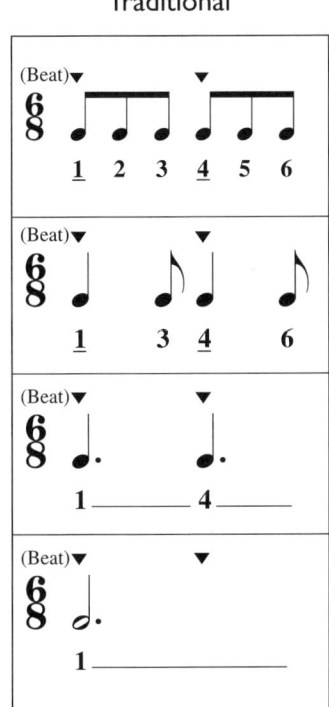
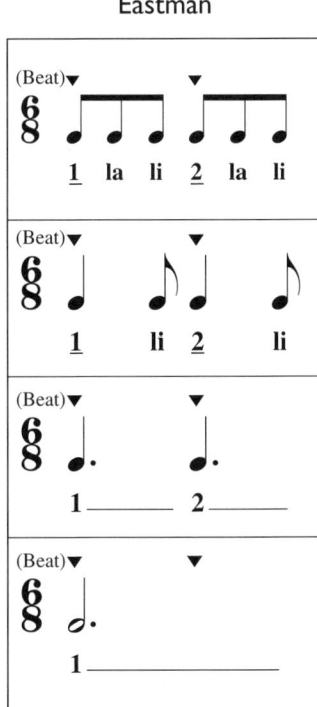

Other Compound Meters

Adapt the information from the above charts to apply to music in other compound meters.

To determine the note that receives the beat, add three divisions together. For example:

6 = Six divisions per measure (♫♩ ♫♩).
8 = The eighth note (♪) receives the division, dotted quarter note (♩.) receives the beat.

9 = Nine divisions per measure (♫♩ ♫♩ ♫♩).
8 = The eighth note (♪) receives the division, dotted quarter note (♩.) receives the beat.

12 = Twelve divisions per measure (♩♩♩ ♩♩♩ ♩♩♩ ♩♩♩).
4 = The quarter note (♩) receives the division, dotted half note (♩.) receives the beat.

An exception to this compound meter rule is when the music occurs at a slow tempo, then the music is felt in beats, rather than divisions.